Don't Wait For Me

a novel by

DAN KOLBET

Copyright © 2012 Dan Kolbet

All rights reserved.

ISBN 1480080659
ISBN-13 978-1480080652

For Katie, Allison and Felicity.

Dan Kolbet

One

Black Friday: 30 days until Christmas Eve

Edwin sat behind his desk in the windowless back room of his toy store, Mr. Z's. His antique wooden chair squeaked with his every movement. A bare bulb illuminated the jumbled room. His coffee cup, a red mug with a snowman painted on it, sat before him. He took gentle sips and let the burn of the bourbon sting his throat. He'd ditched the coffee at noon and it was now well past seven o'clock.

The store's daily receipts were in four neat piles on the desktop. Small piles. Very small piles. Today was not his Black Friday and he resented the common notion that this one blasted day was the one that would bring his store out of the red and back into the black. Back into the black? The store was losing money hand over fist.

But today's terrible showing wasn't a surprise. Not a surprise to Edwin or for the handful of customers who came into the store today. The regulars knew it shouldn't have been him behind the glass display case, ringing up their precious purchases.

One exceedingly talkative customer happened to ask the question he dreaded, but expected every day.

"Where's Mary and Mr. Z?"

His reply gave no satisfaction to the customer buying an electric train set. But of course, the answer gave Edwin no satisfaction either, so it all balanced out in his mind. He'd been asking the same question for 10 months and two days. Where's Mary?

Of Mr. Z, he was more certain—he'd been dead for years, but people still asked.

But the receipts and the annoying customer questions weren't dominating his disdain at this exact moment. It was the shoplifter sitting in the folding chair directly across from the desk.

"When can I go home?" the boy asked for the third time in the last five minutes.

"I told you," Edwin said. "The police should be here any minute. Now keep quiet I'm trying to count."

"You've got a lot of crap back here. You should really clean up," the boy said.

"That's quite a recommendation from a thief," Edwin said.

"I told you I would pay for it."

"It's customary to pay for something at the time it leaves the store, not halfway down the block."

The boy had entered the store about 5:30 p.m. The bell above the door gave a ring as he walked right by Edwin, who was straightening a shelf of puzzles near the register. The boy's green canvas jacket, with large pockets, immediately drew Edwin's attention away from the puzzles and toward the boy, who was probably no older than 10. With his dark cap, covered in fresh snow, Edwin couldn't judge his age very well at all.

Big pockets. No parents. Shifty eyes. Did he have shifty eyes? Of course he did. They all do. If it wasn't the damn economy, big box stores or websites stealing his customers—it was shoplifters who would certainly be the end of this business. And he caught one—finally.

But the joy of catching the little thief in the act was spoiled by the long wait for the police to show up. No doubt there were bigger crimes that needed investigating, but he had the criminal in the back room. Caught him red-handed. If the cops would just show up and arrest him already, Edwin could go home or to the Satellite Diner for a late dinner.

It wasn't lost on Edwin that this little boy was the only person he'd had an actual conversation with in months. Excluding his few customers, he couldn't recall the last time he had spent so much time together with another person inside the store since Mary had gone. A sad state of affairs, indeed. Edwin desperately wanted this day just to be over.

If he hadn't turned the corner just in time to see the boy drop a Barbie swimsuit and surfboard combo pack into his coat pocket, he wouldn't still be sitting at his desk right now.

"What do you want with a Barbie anyway?" Edwin asked the boy.

"None of your business," the boy said.

"Actually it is my business. All 2,100 square feet of it."

"And what a great job you've done with the place," the boy deadpanned.

Great, even this little punk knows I'm a failure, Edwin thought.

* * *

After several more calls to the police department it became apparent they weren't coming to haul the kid to the slammer. He didn't even know if they did that anymore. Probably they would just give him a stern talking to and take him to his parents.

Edwin figured he could be just as imposing as a police officer – especially one who never showed up. He could scare this kid straight. So he decided he'd get the boy to his parents and let them decide his punishment. He could imagine the embarrassment on their faces, finding out their sweet little boy was a future master criminal. He was actually looking forward to it. He didn't really like kids, at least not recently.

"Put on your coat, you're going home."

"Hold on there, man, you can't take me to my apartment."

"So, it's an apartment? That's a good start. What's the address?"

"No really. I'll do anything. Please don't take me home."

The kid, with his pleading, seemed to grow younger the more he begged Edwin to not return him home. For a split second Edwin thought he had detected fear in the boy's eyes. Good, I'm still intimidating, he thought.

"It's either the police station or your parents, kid," Edwin said, in his best authoritative tone. "There are no other options. Besides, I couldn't just kick you out onto the street now anyway, it's dark and snowing and you're a little kid."

"Hey, I'll be 11 in January," the boy replied, as if his age was the deciding factor.

"Eleven-year-olds are still little kids."

"It beats being a hundred like you," the boy said.

"Good one, kid. Now put your coat on. I'm taking you home."

Two

Lloyd Zimmerman and his wife Harriet opened Mr. Z's Toys, or more simply Mr. Z's, on the corner of Riverside and Howard, in the heart of downtown Spokane, Washington, in 1968. The store, with its fine selection of children's toys and games, became a Spokane institution. The big green Z on the marquee was even noted in the background of paintings done by local artists and regularly mentioned in tourist brochures.

The Z fell into place next to the city's other well-known landmarks—the Riverfront Park Pavilion, the clock tower and of course the Spokane River falls by Monroe Street.

When people thought of downtown Spokane, they saw the Z and for decades the Z was a smashing success. Christmas was when Lloyd and Harriet shined brightest. They would personally welcome each shopper and help them pick out just the right gift—no matter the budget.

"A simple gift is the best," Lloyd would say. "The cost—high or low—means little, when it comes from the heart. Giving the gift is extra special."

It was this mentality that made their customers feel welcome and made them return time and time again. The couple ran the store alone, with only the occasional part-time employee pitching in during the busy season. But the couple didn't like hiring for those jobs because it meant they wouldn't be able to personally help each customer.

"It was a fool's idea," Harriet had once said. "But our customers are like family to us. And you can't outsource that, can you?"

After years together, the couple had a daughter. Mary. The three Zimmermans were happy. As soon as Mary was tall enough to reach the bottom shelves, she was put to work in the store. At first there was little she could do but entertain the customers with her smile and constant giggling.

As Mary grew older, she was given more responsibility. After school she would take the bus downtown to relieve her mother. This responsibility multiplied when Harriet was diagnosed with late-stage breast cancer. She fought with everything she had, but the disease was swift and ruthless. Harriet succumbed when Mary was a junior in high school.

More than 600 people, including Spokane's mayor, a congressman and hundreds of customers who had been buying toys from her since they were kids, attended the funeral. Mary and Lloyd sat in the front row as dozens and dozens of people came to the front of the church to tell stories about Harriet. Nearly every story took place inside Mr. Z's.

It was the simple things that made people feel good about visiting the store. People marveled over the grace and earnestness with which Harriet set about stocking the store's tall wooden shelves and beautifully decorating the store to match every holiday and seasonal change. Harriet didn't use bar codes, but rather simple price tags written by hand. What they wouldn't say is that they came to the store for a sense of nostalgia—a forgotten age of retail. Mr. Z's didn't sell video games or bicycles, just toys and games that inspired their customers and the child within.

But it wasn't just the toys inside the store that brought people back to another era. It was Harriet's window displays. Each Christmas, without fail, Harriet would decorate the large windows that faced north onto Riverside Avenue. There were years of snowmen sledding and elves working at the North Pole. Santa was a popular performer who was seen sliding out of a chimney or driving the sleigh. Every year a new and special scene was built along those windows. The local newspaper, The Chronicle, would always do at least a small story and print a photograph of the display. That always drew people in.

As Harriet was laid to rest, people wondered who would do Mr. Z's windows? Was her daughter Mary up for the task? What would happen to Mr. Z's now that Harriet was gone?

Three

Amelia Cook pulled the garland down over the outer edges of the curtain rod to frame her apartment's small window that faced the inner courtyard of the low-rent complex. She'd found the garland at a thrift store in North Spokane last week and topped it off with a strand of multi-colored twinkle lights. The plastic garland sparkled when she plugged it in and she took just a moment to admire it before setting about the rest of the holiday decorating. It wouldn't take her long. The two-bedroom apartment didn't have much room for actual decorations, so she made do with whatever she had.

Cotton balls made for a fine blanket of snow surrounding a manger scene made of Lego's. A set of thick red candles, that smelled of summer and fruit punch, became a cute centerpiece above the television when she wrapped the edges with snowflakes made of construction paper. That particular decoration wasn't Amelia's doing alone. Her daughter, 6-year-old Susanna, had helped with the snowflakes. Their jagged edges were perfect, she thought.

"Store bought decorations don't hold a candle to your creations," she said to Susanna.

"Hold a candle?" the little one asked.

"It's a saying," she said.

"What's a saying?"

"I'm saying your snowflakes are the best. No two are alike."

"Just like the real ones?"

"Exactly like the real ones."

Amelia pulled the three-foot tree out of the entryway closet and frowned. A fake tree. Susanna liked to call it their arty-fishy tree because the word 'artificial' doesn't just roll off the tongue for everyone. She wished they could afford a real tree. Not this rubbery two-piece monstrosity with a metal rod in the middle. But it would have to do. And she was sure to place a smile on her face when she showed the arty-fishy tree to Susanna.

"I think you should put it in the kitchen," Susanna said.

"Not the front window?"

Susanna shook her head no.

"That way we can see it when we eat," Susanna said.

"How about we put it in the living room so Santa knows where to find it."

"He wouldn't find it in the kitchen?" Susanna asked.

"He's fickle."

"Pickle?"

"Yes, Santa is a pickle," Amelia said with a smile.

"Then maybe we should leave it by the window, Mommy."

"You're the boss."

Amelia pulled a metal TV tray out from behind the couch and set the tree on top of it. It was a bit tipsier than she'd have liked but at least the neighbors could see it when they glanced up to the second floor. Better to share the season than leave it hidden on the floor for just them to see.

Susanna handed her mother silver and blue mirrored balls from a cardboard box for decorating the tree. It didn't take many to fill it up. The balls that had lost their hooks since the previous Christmas were affixed with paperclips. Hooks weren't the only things they had lost in the move to Spokane from Bonners Ferry, a small town in North Idaho. But she wasn't going to spend time thinking about that now. Not during Christmas. She plugged in the multi-colored lights and they both watched as the lights danced in rhythm with the twinkling lights on the makeshift garland above the window.

"We did it," Amelia said.

"No! Unplug the lights!" Susanna turned and ran into her bedroom before her mother had a chance to ask why.

She returned seconds later with a small package wrapped in white paper.

"We have to put it on," she said.

Amelia opened the package. Inside was a clay giraffe ornament with a circle cut out of its oversized stomach for a picture. Amelia could tell the edges of the giraffe were pressed down with familiar fingers. A band of yarn was strung through the neck for hanging.

"We made it at school," she said. "The giraffe makes our tree tall!"

"I guess you're right."

Amelia inspected the crayon-drawn picture glued to the giraffe's stomach. The tiny scene showed a man and woman flanked by a slightly shorter boy and Susanna herself, drawn significantly larger than the three others. Her curly blonde hair sprang out in every direction. Tiny Susanna tended to draw herself as a giant in all her family drawings, which her mother thought was adorable, while her teachers said it could become an issue in the future. *Teachers. What do they know?*

Amelia couldn't help but smile at the drawing, but it also made her insides hurt at the same time. The picture showed a complete family - Dad included. Susanna couldn't comprehend the complex nature of her parent's relationship, or why Daddy recently moved to Reno, Nevada, and left them behind. Amelia rubbed her finger where a wedding ring should be, but had never been. She couldn't let herself dwell on it. Not today. She had to think of the kids.

"Don't you think you should have given your brother some hair in the picture?" Amelia asked.

"No. He always has a hat on."

"Yes, and I'd rather he didn't."

"Boys will be bees," Susanna said, shrugging her shoulders.

"Boys will be boys," Amelia corrected.

"I know Mom," Susanna said, completely missing the difference.

There was a knock at the apartment door and Susanna ran to answer it.

"Honey, don't open the door unless I'm there," Amelia said, but she could hear the seal on the door pull open before she could round the corner into the hall.

Standing at the doorway was a handsome man in his late 30s in a winter parka. His light blue eyes drew her in immediately. So much so that she didn't even glance at his short companion in the hat—her son, Marcus.

Four

Edwin took a slight step back when the door opened, while his young companion walked right in.

"Can I help you?" Amelia asked. She was tall and slim with blonde hair. She was a very pretty woman, but the concerned look on her face made her seem older than he imagined her to be. He guessed she was in her early 30s.

"Your son stole a doll from my store," he said.

She rolled her eyes in a way that said this wasn't the first time she'd heard of this behavior. She turned and yelled back into the apartment.

"Marcus, get back here!"

The boy returned with a sheepish look on his face.

"You stole a doll?" She asked. "What do you need with a doll?"

Edwin found the question to be somewhat odd. He expected it to be something like, "Why did you steal anything?"

Marcus reached into his coat and pulled out the Barbie swimsuit, surfboard combo pack and held it up for his mom.

"It was for Susanna," he said, as if that explained it all.

A little girl with wild blonde hair rounded the corner and snatched the doll from Marcus' hand, giggled some sort of thank you to all three of them and then disappeared as fast as she came.

Edwin had to stifle a laugh. He'd caught the boy stealing once, but hadn't thought to check his coat again for the doll as they left the store to come to the apartment. His investigative skills were sorely lacking.

"To your room, now," she said to Marcus. "I'll deal with you in a minute."

"But mom, I was going to—"

"Enough. To your room. Now."

Marcus dropped his coat on the floor and stomped past his mother into the apartment.

"I'm sorry Mr.—"

"Edwin. Edwin Klein," he said. "I own Mr. Z's downtown."

"And it's a doll store?" she asked.

"Um, no. Toys and games mostly. You haven't heard of it?"

"We just recently moved to Spokane, from Bonners Ferry. I'm still learning the area."

He nodded.

"Well, Edwin, I sincerely apologize for my son," Amelia said. Her voice was deflated and tired. "He's been going through some personal issues lately and I just haven't been able to . . . well, I just haven't kept an eye on him like I should."

"So this isn't the first time?" Edwin asked.

"I wish I could say it was, but I've made more than one trip to the mall to pick him up after a store calls."

Edwin silently chastised himself for not thinking of that first. Why did he have to drive him home? He should have just called and saved himself a trip to this shabby apartment complex on the north side of town. He made a mental note for next time.

"I just want to make sure he will get a proper punishment," Edwin said. "These sorts of things can lead to bigger crimes with kids like that. Who knows what—"

She cut him off mid-sentence.

"Do you have children, Edwin?"

"No, I don't."

"Well then let me key you in on something that you should understand about kids," she said. Her eyes narrowed intently and she tilted her head slightly to the right. "They mess up. They do things you don't want them to do. They embarrass you. They bring you pain nearly as often as they bring you joy. They aren't perfect. Bigger crimes? That's a laugh. He's a boy and he will be severely punished for what he did, but don't you dare claim to know 'kids like that.'"

"Well, I just meant that—" Edwin stammered.

"I know what you meant," she spat the words at him. "Thank you for bringing him home safely. Merry freaking Christmas."

Her hand was shaking when she slammed the door in his face.

***

Edwin stared at the closed door for a good five seconds wondering how he, and not the sarcastic shoplifter, was the one who wound up with the lecture. He knew kids, at least the ones that came into his store alone. He watched them pawing his merchandise and then leaving without buying anything. They were pocketing something, he was sure of that. It starts with something small, then the next thing you know, these kids are robbing convenience stores. This mother just needed to know where her son was headed. She was lucky Edwin caught him this soon. Crazy woman. Slamming the door in his face.

He descended the steps and cut across the courtyard toward his decade-old Nissan Sentra parked in the lot. It was snowing pretty heavily and he had a hard time finding the pathway through the dark courtyard, which must have been the reason the boy walked around the outside of the building when they arrived at the apartment.

Before he got to the other side of the courtyard he stopped to maneuver around a snow shovel that had been left in the walkway. After placing it against a wall, he turned and looked up at the building he'd just left. It was dark except for one window on the second floor that was surrounded by blinking lights. The star on the top of a Christmas tree just barely poked up to the center of the window.

The backlit figure of a woman stood next to the tree. Her hands covered her face. From the shaking of her shoulders Edwin could clearly see she was sobbing.

He felt ashamed for watching her. Seeing her pain. But he didn't look away for a long while.

And he never even asked her name.

Five

Edwin awoke the next morning to the sounds of his neighbor Jonas shouting at the garbage truck, which for the second week in a row had failed to stop at his driveway for curbside pick-up. The city had instituted Saturday pick-up because they couldn't get all the cans picked up during the week. Jonas flung some select curse words in the general direction of the truck and the city worker at the wheel. Edwin glanced out the window to see Jonas, his bathrobe flapping in the wind, waving his arms like a madman. The rhythmic beep of the truck backing up signaled that the driver heard the shouts or more likely saw Jonas' pasty white legs and took pity on the man.

It's no wonder the driver missed the can as it was obscured by great mounds of snow that Jonas had cleared from his driveway and sidewalk with his oversized snow blower. It hadn't stopped snowing since Thanksgiving night and Jonas had been out clearing walkways ever since. People had started to call it the Turkey Blizzard, which a TV weatherman thought was funny because it sounded like turkey gizzard. But just days after Thanksgiving the funniness had worn off a bit. Schools had closed and the city had declared a snow emergency, asking drivers to park on one side of the street or the other to ensure the plows could clear the streets. It was a novel idea for Spokane at the time, but few people listened and the streets were as difficult to navigate as they ever had been.

Edwin had seen snowy Spokane winters before, having lived in or just outside the city his entire life. The white stuff rarely shut down the city, but this year's constant barrage was a pretty good excuse indeed. Unfortunately, that meant even fewer shoppers at Mr. Z's. When all was said and done, sales were down about 35 percent from the previous year's sales. The special advertisements in the newspaper and comical jingles on the radio hadn't brought in the customers promised by the insistent media sales people either. The store was sinking.

He stopped in the hallway outside of his bedroom to look at a framed picture. It was of a much younger Edwin. Happy, content and oblivious to the realities of the world. He was sitting atop a magnificent brown mare. The horse, named Scout, had white socks that extended halfway up his legs. Edwin used to spend extra time after each ride washing down the horse's legs—more than he really needed to—so the brilliant white color would shine through. Edwin recalled the day the picture was taken. He was 12 and barely old enough to help his neighbor, Mr. Debre, take care of his stables. His mom had taken the picture.

In exchange for riding lessons, Edwin would work in the stables. Truth be told, he was working for pennies on the dollar, but he didn't care. He just wanted to ride and he was good at it too. By the time he graduated high school he was a full-time ranch hand being paid a traditional wage.

Edwin's responsibilities rose as Mr. Debre's health began to decline. Edwin had dreamed of one day taking over the stables and turning the rundown place into a world-class facility. There was enough land to make it work and definitely a need. People would drop by all the time looking to ride. There was also a small customer base that boarded their horses at the stables.

So when Mr. Debre passed on, Edwin mourned the man, but quietly waited to find out what would happen to the stables. His disappointment couldn't have hit him harder. Mr. Debre's children sold the house, stables, land and animals. The horses Edwin had cared for since he was a boy, were scattered every which way. The new owners just wanted the land and the house, not the stables and certainly not a ranch hand who had no formal training.

He tried to get on at other stables and ranches, but his lack of official training meant it would be years before he could work his way to the top again. His wages would be too low even by Mr. Debre's standards. And by that time he was engaged to be married to Mary Zimmerman, the toy store owner's daughter. He needed an income that would support a wife and hopefully a family. So he set his dreams aside and got a 9-to-5 job selling used cars, while taking a few college courses here and there. It paid the bills while Mary finished school, but it certainly wasn't as gratifying as working the stables. Not by a mile.

Edwin stopped staring at the picture in his hallway and forced himself to stop thinking about the past too. As he showered and shaved, he admitted to himself that he was dreading going in to the store. Couldn't he also take a snow day? The rest of the city had. Why not him? But he knew why. He couldn't miss a day because of Mary. She wouldn't have let him miss a day and he wasn't going to let her down. Not again. Thoughts of her filled his mind and he could feel his heart pumping harder in his chest. The same damaged heart that started this whole mess. He steadied himself on the bathroom counter knowing if his heartbeat elevated he'd have to sit and let it calm down to avoid passing out—or worse. Damn heart.

If not for his heart, Mary would still be here, he thought.

* * *

The city workers had cleared the Riverside Avenue sidewalk in front of Mr. Z's, which was a welcome change from the previous days when Edwin had to shovel pathways himself. Not that he was entirely opposed to doing the work himself, but he'd rather be indoors where it was warm. The sight of the clear walkway as he approached from a distance actually put a smile on his face—the first one all morning.

The smile didn't last long.

The first sign of trouble came when Edwin realized the city hadn't in fact cleared the sidewalk of snow, but rather poured a thick layer of ice on it that snaked around the footing of the building. As he skated around the corner of the building he wondered why in the world the sidewalk was a sheet of ice. Nowhere else on his walk in to work did he see such a thing.

The ice sheet seemed to be getting rougher as he got closer to the door. At the threshold, he lost his footing completely, slammed his stomach into a parking meter by the curb and fell flat on his back, whacking his head on the ground. From this position the big green "Z" on the store sign was directly overhead, shrouded in misty fog. But it wasn't fog at all; it was steam. In fact all of the store's windows were filled with steam.

He carefully got to his feet while pulling his keys out of his pocket to unlock the front door. The latch opened easily, but as he pushed the door inward, it was a struggle. A thick layer of slush filled the entryway. He stomped up the two inner steps, making footprints in the slush. When he got to the register he could survey the entire store. It was flooded with water. Tiny streams had formed over frozen pockets so that the water was swirling around the shelves and out the front steps like a racetrack.

He moved down each aisle, surveying the damage and trying to find the source of the water, which seemed to be coming from beneath the floor itself. He couldn't piece it together. The old wooden floor, which had worn smooth through years of footfalls was bathed in a wet sheen and little icebergs.

It's ruined. How could I let this happen? He wondered.

He started to feel lightheaded near the stuffed animals and went down to his knees in front of a rack of plastic dinosaurs. The last thing he saw before he finally fainted was Mary herself standing in the doorway with a blue box resting in both hands.

Mary?

His face fell into a slight dip in the floor that had formed a puddle. Water continued to pour in, quickly covering his mouth as everything went black.

Six

Two Years Earlier

"I'm taking your place and that's final," Mary demanded. Tears streaked down her face as she pushed Edwin away. She knew what needed to be done just as he did.

"That's not the deal we made," he said. "I signed up. I'm supposed to go."

"Tell that to your heart defect," she said.

As soon as she said it she'd wished she could take it back. She knew how much it would hurt.

"Babe, I'm sorry, that's not what I meant," she said.

He was angry, but so was she. They both knew this was the wrong time to discuss it, emotions were too high, but they had a pact since the day they got married to never put off an argument for another day. Just have it out. Even on a day like this.

"We don't need the bonus money that bad," he said. "We'll figure it out. No more talk of you signing up. There's real fighting happening overseas. You can't go there."

"I didn't even want you to go, remember?" she said. "I begged you not to do it and now you're telling me that I can't take your place?"

"I just don't want to see you get hurt," he said.

"It's just the Army Reserves," she said, but she knew the danger.

"The Reserves get deployed too, you know."

She was trying to hold it together, but a quiver crept into her voice.

"It's $20,000 to enlist," she said, repeating the figure they both knew so well. "We already spent that money when we thought you'd be getting it. If I don't sign up and get that money, we won't make it through the summer. We'll lose the store, the house—everything."

"We can make it a little longer," he said, desperate to convince her that there was some other way. "I know we can. We can sell the Mr. Z's building if we have to. Those developers want that corner lot."

"No, Edwin," she said, defiantly. "Why would you even bring that up? I'm not closing my parent's store. I don't care how much money they offer. It's our responsibility now. They worked seven days a week for four decades at that store. I can't let it fail a year after it became ours."

"Your father knew the place was on the downhill when he passed," he said. "It hadn't turned a profit in five years. It barely broke even."

"It doesn't matter. I'm not selling," she said. "We're going to make this store work. This money is going to help us get back on our feet and we're going to be able to keep the house."

"There are still a few banks I haven't called yet," he said, but it wasn't true. He'd called them all.

"The answer is going to be no, just like the dozen that said no before," she said. "Nobody is lending to little mom-and-pop's anymore. We're not getting a loan."

Edwin had feared that Mary would offer herself up when the doctor told him that he had something wrong with his heart and he needed more tests. He'd always had a bit of a "tricky heart," but he'd shrugged it off as undiagnosed asthma or just being tired. So when the final word came down that the Army wouldn't take him, he wasn't surprised. He wanted to wait to tell Mary. To try and figure something out before she volunteered herself, but as soon as he saw her that night he couldn't hold back his own tears. He told her immediately.

It was always that way between them. No matter the issue, they worked through it together. They couldn't keep anything from the other. Which was the main reason Edwin argued so hard with her to not join up. He knew she was right, they needed the money and there wasn't anything he or his damn heart could do to stop her.

Seven

Present Day

The streams of ice and water continued to pool up on the store's wooden floor as Edwin lay motionless in front of the plastic dinosaur display. A T-Rex floated by, gently bumping against his shoulder. His face remained buried in a large pool of water. He wasn't breathing, even as his mind drifted. For a split second Edwin considered what it would mean to stay in the puddle. To not take another breath. But by instinct, he tried to breathe and choked on a mouthful of water.

It seemed so easy to just lay his head back down as the icy waters soothed him to sleep. But that was ridiculous, he thought. He pushed the idea back down inside himself, embarrassed that it floated to the surface. He rolled over, bringing himself back to reality. He lifted his head and sucked in another mouthful of air. This time the air filled his lungs, expanding his chest. He was slowly becoming more alert.

Where was Mary? Hadn't he seen her in the doorway? Did she wake him? But that simply wasn't possible. Then he saw the woman with the blue box.

She was standing at the front door talking to a man in white coveralls named Chang. After a few moments the man left and the woman turned. Edwin sat up and leaned against the dinosaurs. At first he didn't recognize her. He couldn't tell where he'd seen her before, until she spoke.

"It seems you have a water problem," she said with a slight smile. It was the mother of the master criminal he'd caught shoplifting on Black Friday. Was she happy about his misfortune? She was remarkably upbeat.

"I gathered as much," he said with a deep sigh.

"The guy from the Laundromat behind your store said his reserve hot water holding tank burst overnight," she said. "Apparently you share a common ventilation system. He said they didn't find the leak until this morning because the backflow came in here, not his Laundromat."

Chang's Laundromat had been open for business for nearly as long as Mr. Z's. Edwin didn't know Mr. Chang well, but they often said good morning to one another on the street before opening their businesses for the day. Chang always paid his rent for the leased space in the building and that was enough for Edwin.

"The least he could have done was turn it off," he said, throwing his hands in air and flinging water on Amelia. The water that Edwin remained sitting in, was still streaming out the front door.

"They had to call someone from the city to come out and turn it off," she said. "He is there now working on it."

As if on cue, the sound of running water in the walls of the store stopped and the streams of water quickly turned to a trickle. Edwin hadn't registered the sound until it was gone.

"Let me help you up," she said.

She lifted Edwin to his feet and the two of them walked around the store surveying the damage. All the merchandise on the lower shelves was soaked. Books, puzzles and stuffed animals were all dripping wet. The water on the floor had started to settle into large puddles.

Edwin recalled the first time he'd been asked to clean the floor. It was roughly five years prior when he dropped his other jobs and came to work at the store full-time. Mr. Zimmerman left for the night, but asked that the floors be done after closing time. Edwin had filled a bucket with water, dumped in some pine-scented floor cleaner he found in the employee restroom and dunked a large mop in the suds. He had just slapped the wet mop on the floor when a shriek came from the doorway of the backroom.

"Pick that up," Mary had said, with a panic in her voice. "You can't mop these floors, they don't have a finish on them. It'll warp the wood."

Edwin and Mary had tried to dry the wet area as best they could, but the floor warped quickly after it dried, causing a small tripping hazard in front of the remote-control airplanes and sailboats.

* * *

As he looked around at the totality of today's drenching of the entire floor, he wished for the small tripping hazard by the airplanes and sailboats. This damage was devastating. The floor was already becoming soft as a sponge. As he walked it sucked at his shoes. It would take days to dry completely and even after it dried the floor would be nearly impassable given the certainty of warping. The last thing Edwin needed was to be cited by the city for having a hazardous floor.

He spun in a circle with his hands raised to his head, just taking it all in, when he remembered that he wasn't alone in the store. The woman with the blue box balanced on her upturned palms—Marcus' mom—was leaning against the counter, watching him and his visible torment.

She noticed his attention.

"I owe you $11.46," she said.

"Huh?"

"For Barbie and her surfboard," she said. "The one my son meant to pay for."

"Right, thanks," he said, eyeing the blue box.

This was all he could muster to say. He was afraid that saying more would incite another parental lecture. Seeing how the day was already going so well, he decided it best to avoid her wrath.

"I didn't realize that we kept the doll until after you left that night," she said. "I'm sorry about that. I took it out of Marcus' allowance and wrapped it up. It will be under the tree on Christmas morning."

"It's OK."

"And I wanted to let you know that Marcus has been grounded from his video games and television for two weeks. He'll also be stopping by later to do any chores you might have around the store."

"I don't know if there's anything for him to do," Edwin said. "Just look at this place. I'll have to shut it down. I never thought it would end like this."

"There are companies that specialize in this sort of thing. I think they call it disaster recovery. Your insurance should cover it."

"Not in time for Christmas," he said. He rubbed his temples with both hands. "I won't likely see a check from them until the New Year and by then there'll be nothing left to recover from this disaster. If I can't stay open in December, I'm through."

He explained the warping of the floors and his precarious financial situation. He hated to take such a defeatist stance, but the situation was dire by all accounts.

"So it seems to me that you have three options," she said. "First—you could just give up, lose your business and sit on your warped floor as the bank repossesses all your merchandise, hopes and dreams."

"That doesn't sound very inviting," Edwin said.

"Good. It shouldn't," she said. "Second—you can call your insurance company and hope you get a good agent who can get you back on your feet quickly. Considering the time of year that might be a tough sell."

"I agree with you on that one," he said, thinking option three had to be better than the first two, but wondering why he was even entertaining this woman's ideas. "So, what's option three?"

"Hiring me, right now," she said, a grin spreading across her face.

"Hiring you for what?"

"You might not think it to look at me, but I'm pretty handy," she said. "I have a feeling that we can dry these floors out with some commercial propane hot air driers and sand them down with a rented wood sander in just a few days. It won't be perfect, but it should be enough to get your doors open again."

"What about all this merchandise?" he said, picking up a stuffed teddy bear that dripped back onto the floor. "What's your plan for that."

"Hey, you're the boss," she said. "I'm just an employee."

"So you've hired yourself now?"

"It seems that way," she said.

"I don't even know your name."

"Amelia Cook," she said. "Now, enough talking. Let's get to work."

She stuck out her hand. Edwin started to reach out for it, but caught himself. What exactly was he doing? He didn't even know this woman and now he's going to trust her with his store's future?

She continued to hold out her hand. Watching him.

"I don't bite," she said. "Promise."

He shook her hand.

"What's in the box?" he asked.

She pealed back the lid to reveal a homemade pumpkin pie.

"I wanted to say thank you for bringing Marcus home that night," she said. "You didn't have to go to all that trouble."

He hadn't had homemade pumpkin pie for years because Mary hated it and refused to make it.

"Thank you," he said, taking the pie and smiling to himself. "Now, let's get to work."

Eight

Readying the store for customers took three full days. The propane-fed commercial air dryers made quick work of the wet flooring, at least on the surface. The subfloor beneath the planks of wood was still wet and likely wouldn't dry completely for another day or two. Amelia was concerned the water would create a musty smell, but she didn't tell Edwin. He had enough to worry about already.

The warped floor made for an annoying amount of speed bumps for little Susanna's Barbie Corvette that she raced up and down the aisles. After the dryers were returned to the rental shop, Susanna had come with her mom to work on cleaning up the store. Of course, it was a toy store after all, so her version of work involved testing out every toy in the place, much to Edwin's chagrin. But the little girl was growing on him, even if he wouldn't admit it.

Amelia was certain that a rough sanding of the floor, hard shaving on some high spots, plus a little wood filler on some particularly large gaps would bring the floor into proper shape. Edwin delegated the floor work to Amelia, knowing that his involvement would just be a hindrance to progress. He was more concerned about the thousands of dollars worth of ruined merchandise—most of which was purchased on credit.

Small musical instruments, princess and cowboy dress-up clothes and various art supplies lay soaked beside action figures and model trains in a sad-looking garbage bin.

"None of this stuff is salvageable?" Amelia asked.

"It's not retail-ready, so we can't sell it," he said. "Nobody wants to buy a toy in a crumpled cardboard box. The stuffed animals could be washed and dried, but they would only sell for a fraction of what I paid for them wholesale. Used toys? It wouldn't be worth it."

Amelia couldn't believe the waste.

"So it's all trash?" she asked.

"Pretty much," he said. "I cataloged everything to submit to the insurance company, but I won't come close to breaking even."

Edwin was thankful the flood only impacted the lower shelves. All the merchandise above floor level remained dry. Edwin surveyed the lost goods and tried to calculate how much these items would pull the store further into the red. Being closed over the last three days was bad enough. The store worked on a razor-thin margin as it was, but at the moment his margin was beginning to mold in the garbage bin.

* * *

On the second day of cleanup, Edwin left Amelia and Susanna alone in the store. He had arranged a meeting with a bank to discuss a line of credit. He gathered his papers in a briefcase and headed out into another snowstorm, walking just a few blocks down to a local bank branch where he thought the manager might be favorable to him. The store had a long history with the main bank, but the nearest local branch was on the same street as Mr. Z's and that had to count for something.

He seemed determined to succeed, Amelia thought, despite all the setbacks. She'd seen his drive over the past few days as they worked side by side. The line of credit was a long shot this late in the year, he'd told her as he left, but he had to try.

The floor sander was supposed to arrive late that afternoon, so Amelia agreed to stay in the store even though there really wasn't anything left for her to do. The soaked toys had been removed from the shelves, while the remaining inventory had been spread out to fill the space. She had never had a job in a retail store before, but to her eyes, the shelves looked great—yet Edwin kept fiddling with them.

He had an eye for little details in the store, even if he didn't seem happy about it. She'd watched him, trying to learn what it took to run the small business. Her own professional work experience was very limited. She'd been waitressing since high school at a diner in Bonners Ferry. She'd progressed as much as any waitress could expect in a small town, which wasn't that far at all. She got her pick of shifts, which was good since she had two kids at home to tend to early in the morning and at night when they couldn't go do daycare or school. Being a single mother wasn't easy, but she viewed her children as a blessing. Her saving grace was that her older sister Amy owned the diner, so she could come and go as she needed.

Josh Martin, Marcus and Susanna's father, was the all-too-typical athlete who peaked in high school. The former high school quarterback blew his scholarship to the University of Montana when he was caught drinking at a party. This one mistake held him captive in Bonners Ferry for years. He was a good man who supported his kids by working construction jobs. He and Amelia stayed together for the kids, but never got married. The spark just kept going out. There was no question that she loved him and he loved her, but it rarely seemed to occur at the same time, even as they raised the kids together under the same roof.

Just 18 months ago, an opportunity was presented to the couple that they thought would forever change their situation. Both of them desperately wanted to get out of Bonners Ferry, but they just didn't have the means or, until then, the will to get on with it. Josh had been accepted into the Pre-Apprentice Electric Line School program in Spokane.

He asked Amelia, Susanna and Marcus to move down to Spokane too while he was in school. After six months, he said he'd have a great job as a utility linemen starting at about $45,000 a year—enough to support them all. It was a mountain of money to people who had seen very little in their lifetimes. Maybe Amelia could go back to school too, Josh had said. She'd taken some computer classes online, but didn't come close to finishing a degree program.

It was an easy decision to pack up and move to Spokane. Marcus protested about leaving his friends and his older cousin Max, but after a few weeks he stopped complaining about missing their old home. The family settled into a routine, one that Amelia was comfortable with. He studied and she worked a waitressing job to support the family. They scrimped and saved everything they had to make it work, but they were in it together.

Amelia let herself think that maybe they could make it work long-term. Maybe they could finally get married. After he got steady work, she thought, the stress of money would be gone and they could focus on their relationship.

But after graduation Josh wasn't offered a job with any local utility company and he learned they wouldn't be hiring again until the next year. This had all happened in the dead of winter so finding a construction job using his old skill set was off the table too. But there were plenty of lineman jobs available—in Nevada. A utility in Reno called and offered him a position over the phone. He accepted the job during that first phone call. He promised her that after he got settled he'd find the whole family a place to live in Reno so they could be together, but Amelia knew better almost immediately.

She knew she'd been fooled—or fooled herself.

She'd supported them in Spokane on her waitressing salary and tips. How else could he afford to attend school if not for her? How would he have lived during those few months? He had to drag all of us to Spokane, she thought.

Several months after he'd moved to Reno, she got the call that he'd found a girlfriend who he planned to marry. There was no place for Amelia in Reno. She didn't hold it against him, at least not too much. She shouldn't have to fight to keep them together, she thought. He should want it too. If they couldn't be happy together, maybe they could be happy apart.

She was on her own with two kids for the first time in her life.

She continued to waitress when she could get hours, going about her day, always counting the minutes until her shift ended and she could see her kids again. She'd briefly considered going back to Bonners Ferry, but the idea of facing her friends and telling them she had failed was too much for her to handle. Spokane was now their home for better or for worse.

Twisting Edwin's arm to hire her at the store meant she had to quit her waitressing job. She hadn't given it a second thought. She saw Edwin, the store and the need and she saw herself in the middle of it. She wanted to be at Mr. Z's. She wanted to be the one to take care of things for once.

Amelia's sister, Amy, had always been the responsible one. Their mother was a drug addict and the elder sister had seen to it that Amelia was cared for. When Josh came along, he watched out for Amelia and the kids. There was always someone. But she was tired of being the weak one. Tired of needing to have a protector. Maybe that's why she jumped into Mr. Z's with both feet, because she was finally needed. She wanted to be needed.

* * *

Amelia entered the toy store's back office in search of an extension cord for the large floor sander that had just arrived. She'd been so busy over the last few days tidying up the rest of the place that she'd yet to venture into this dark area of the store. Edwin kept the door shut and had never invited her to enter.

The smell hit her before she even flipped on the light. A thick, musty odor filled her nostrils and she was forced to turn her head in an attempt to rid herself of the nauseating scent. The room must have flooded, just as the rest of the store had, but for some reason Edwin hadn't cleaned this room out, which was particularly puzzling because he spent so much time in it. Why hadn't he cleaned it? She wasn't sure.

The room was stuffed with a little bit of everything. Stacks of cardboard boxes, reaching as high as the ceiling, leaned in awkward towers toward each other.

Bags of toys and wrapping paper were strewn about the floor. In one far corner the burgundy tip of a reindeer's nose poked out from behind a wooden sleigh that was barely visible behind reels of Christmas lights and boxes of ornaments.

As she looked at a few more closed boxes, careful not to knock them over, she realized the entire backroom was completely filled with unused Christmas decorations. There were more decorations than could possibly fit on display in the store all at once. The outside labels said things like, "Left Mahogany Railing Garland and Lights," or "Gold Angels for the Overhang" or "Chimney for Santa."

When she finally found an extension cord for the sander—connected to a strand of lights—she returned to the store front and for the first time truly noticed that the store showed no signs whatsoever of the holidays. Nothing at all to remind shoppers what brought them into the store—the season of giving. She didn't know much about retail, but she knew how to shop. The decorations helped. These things were important, even in the rush of the holidays when shoppers were more likely to elbow each other out of the way for the last toy truck than to gaze at the seasonal decorations. But today Mr. Z's was just a bare store where it might as well be August.

Amelia peered through the empty store-front windows and saw the horse-drawn carriage that always circulated in downtown Spokane during Christmas time. A half-dozen passengers were departing by a coffee shop. Shiny black metal streetlights were wrapped with large red ribbons and bows, while tiny white lights encircled the sidewalk trees from trunk to tip. Two boys playfully tossed snowballs at each other, while being scolded by their mother for leaving their hot chocolate on the ground. The snow continued to slowly drift downward.

It was a quintessential holiday scene if there ever was one—plenty of smiles and good cheer. Yet Mr. Z's sat warped, empty and devoid of Christmas altogether. Amelia needed to know why.

Nine

Fourteen Months Earlier

Edwin talked while balancing the phone against his shoulder. It was the only way to hand out the Halloween candy to all of the trick-or-treaters and not hang up the phone.

"Yes, I ordered the new display sign," he said.

"Did you pick it out yourself?" Mary asked on the other end of the line. She was in Texas, completing some special Army training program for her Washington National Guard Reserve unit.

"I did not pick it out, just like you asked, dear," he said. He was earnestly following her instructions to the letter. "It was the one you OK'd."

Before leaving for training Mary had made it very clear that any decorating or advertising decisions should be run past her before anything was decided. Mary was pretty obsessive about the way the store looked even from thousands of miles away. Edwin was glad for the help, too. He finally had a good handle on the store's accounting and inventory processes and didn't have the time or willingness to pick the best location for an oversized red bow or mistletoe.

"Did you unpack any of the Christmas boxes yet?"

"You told me not to do that until two weeks after Halloween," he said.

"Just checking," she said, pleased that he'd listened. "I think you're getting the hang of it. And remember you'll know what to do with each box when you open it up. I left you instructions."

"OK, honey."

She'd been reminding him about the boxes since the day she left—or so it seemed. She just wanted the store to look nice and he respected that.

He had yet to unpack any of the boxes, just as Mary had asked, but he'd seen the store in full Christmas mode before and thought he could wing it pretty well if the boxes didn't reveal all, as Mary had promised. She had dutifully labeled each box on the outside with a black marker that included the item for display and its location.

The store window display was an entirely different thing though. The north-facing wall contained a five-foot deep alcove raised two feet off the ground. The display area extended to the top of the windows. The back of the alcove was closed with a glass sliding door so the display area could be accessed. Mary had drawn schematics of where items should be placed and how the animated items had to be plugged in to not overload the store's electrical panel. This year's scene was supposed to be an updated version of a previous season's Christmas village. Handmade houses, storefronts and street vendor kiosks were to span a half-circle around the little village's oversized Christmas tree.

Mary had used construction paper and cardboard to make the buildings but hadn't had time to put them all together, she had told him.

"If you run into trouble, just leave me a message and I'll call you back," she said. "These displays really draw in customers and we need them."

"Don't worry, I've got everything under control, honestly."

He didn't want to talk to her about their money problems. The $20,000 enlistment bonus money was already gone and he was worried about cash flow, but he wouldn't breathe a word of it to her, not while she was away.

"Tell me about your training," he said.

As she provided him a detailed account of her pre-dawn mornings, grueling hot days and sleepless nights, Edwin continued to hand out candy to ghosts and goblins who knocked on his door for a Halloween treat. He listened stoically to his wife, not really soaking in every detail, but just happy to be talking to her, just like it was before she left.

"I've got to go, honey," she said. "I can't call tomorrow because we're doing a training exercise overnight, but I'll text you if I can."

"OK, be careful," he said. "I love you."

"I love you too," she said, pausing for a moment, "more than anything."

"I can't wait to see you."

"It's only a few more months," she said. "I'll be home for Christmas. It'll be just like it was before."

"I'll be waiting for you at the airport the minute your plane lands."

"I'm going to hold you to that."

"I hope you do," he said. He was already counting the days until she returned home to him.

With that, they said their goodbyes.

Edwin dumped the entire candy bowl into the next child's bag, then flipped off the porch and interior lights so no more neighbor kids would knock on the door and see the tears streaking down his face.

Ten

Present Day

The strong wind blew hard against Edwin's face as he stumbled down the sidewalk. His cheeks were impervious to the cold, having been artificially numbed several times already by the bourbon he'd downed in large self-indulgent gulps. He'd always been a social drinker, enjoying a beer or two with friends or at holiday functions, but over the last few months he'd switched to the hard stuff and his drinking was getting out of hand. With no one around to watch his slide into alcoholism, he'd completely missed the transformation himself.

The streets of downtown Spokane were still busy with shoppers and people getting off work. Not that Edwin was paying attention to anyone passing him by on the street. His coat was zipped up tightly around him, but he held it even tighter with his hands in his pockets. He'd left his briefcase of loan papers at the bar. He didn't need those papers anyway, he thought.

His meeting with the banker, Frank Wallace, was a sham—a courtesy to a long-time customer more than an actual business meeting. He needed the credit line to buy inventory to replace what the flood destroyed. If he had nothing to sell, the store didn't have a chance to make a profit. He'd left the bank embarrassed from his situation and his actions.

"If you don't have something to put up for collateral, I'm afraid the bank won't be able to lend you any operating capital Mr. Klein," Wallace said.

Wallace had this same conversation with dozens of business owners over the past few months. He wanted to help, but not if the numbers didn't work. "We've been hit by this economic downturn too and we can't give out money for nothing. You have nothing for collateral?"

Edwin thought of the real estate developer who had offered a small fortune to buy the Mr. Z's building. But that cash would mean no more Mr. Z's. He also couldn't put the building up as collateral because he and Mary had done that before, then defaulted on a loan and nearly lost the building. There was still some equity in the building, but the bank probably wouldn't take the gamble on it anyway.

"No collateral," Edwin said. "The building is off limits."

"What about a home or vehicle?" Wallace said.

"No real equity in the house and the car's a piece of junk," he said. "We need the credit to buy inventory. There's nothing you can do?"

"Like I said before, we aren't a charity. We—"

"So I'm a charity case?" Edwin asked, his face flushing. "Our store has had several accounts with this bank for more than four decades—longer than I've been alive. In all that time not once has a payment been missed. And now that we actually need a little extra help—we're a charity?"

"Sir, I only mean that the very definition of a charity is—"

"Forget you, pal. My mistake," Edwin's voice boomed over the bank lobby. Employees and customers turned to watch. "I thought that loyalty meant something, but apparently I was wrong. I guess it's too much to ask for a little faith in something. I guess 40 years of a partnership didn't earn that right. I'm sorry for wasting your time. I'm sure you need to get back to foreclosing on some little old lady's double-wide trailer or something. I'll see myself out. Thank you very much."

A security guard was already at Wallace's desk when Edwin stood to leave. When the guard put his hand on Edwin's arm to lead him outside, Edwin elbowed him in the stomach by instinct. The guard didn't take kindly to it, and pulled Edwin's wrist in a twist behind his back and pushed him toward the exit doors.

"Don't hurt him," Wallace told the guard. "He's just had a stroke of bad luck."

The fight inside Edwin had flamed out and he didn't resist being ushered outside, humiliated by the whole scene.

Minutes later he found himself at the nearest pub counter, drinking in the late afternoon. People there didn't ask questions or judge him. They just stared at their glasses in between sips. It was quiet and he downed more drinks than he could handle on an empty stomach. He watched the bartender slowly pour more and more drinks. Some of them made their way to him. The world slowed and the alcohol turned his thoughts into a thick molasses haze.

He fumbled with his phone and dialed Mary's cell number from speed dial. No answer. *Oh, that's right, she can't answer.*

Someone plunked quarters into the jukebox and out came Bing Crosby's smooth baritone. He was singing White Christmas with a choir. Whatever Crosby was dreaming of—treetops glistening or sleigh bells in the snow—it didn't have an impact on Edwin or his fellow bar mates. He scanned the place. No one looked up. No one commented on the irony of the buckets of snow clogging the streets and wreaking havoc across town. It was sure to be a white Christmas, but who cares, really? May your days be merry and bright? As if.

"Turn it off," Edwin said.

"What's that, bub?" the bartender asked.

"That song. Turn it off."

"But it's Bing. He's from Spokane. What'da got against Bing?"

"Just turn it to something else."

"Even if I could, I wouldn't. It's Bing," the man said, taking away Edwin's empty glass. "You need another?"

He didn't need another, but he gladly accepted it anyway.

* * *

And so he found himself on the streets again, having left the bar. His numb cheeks battered by the blowing wind that took his breath away. He bumped into a man walking the opposite direction on the sidewalk.

"Watch it, buddy," the man growled. "Drunk idiot."

The man was carrying several bags with wrapped gifts sticking out the tops. Edwin's mind worked slowly for a reply, but by the time something bubbled to the surface, the man and his bags were gone.

"I'm not drunk," he said to no one in particular.

He made it back to his car, but the key wouldn't open it. In fact he didn't know why he parked it there. It was so far from where it should have been. Someone must have moved it, he thought. It didn't occur to him that it wasn't his car.

He gave up on the car and thought about just going to the store, but he didn't want to face that Amelia woman and her perpetual perkiness. There was only so much "upbeat" he could take. He started walking toward his house, forgetting or just not caring that it was a five-mile trek up the South Hill.

He made it a grand total of three blocks before he needed to rest. He found a nice spot across from a McDonald's that looked inviting. He needed to lie down to stop the world from spinning. Just for a minute, he told himself. Overhead a purple neon cross blinked. Edwin didn't notice.

Eleven

Pastor John Isakson was late. The walk from the downtown bus plaza seemed especially long because of the snow. The bus wasn't his first choice, not in this weather. It would have been much quicker to drive. His car had been buried by a city plow earlier that morning and then covered by a fresh layer of snow. By the time he realized that his car was hopelessly trapped in a block of ice, he didn't have the time to dig it out. He needed to get to rehearsal. He couldn't let the kids down. Luckily he was able to catch a bus returning to downtown.

He often enjoyed riding the bus, as so many of his church's congregants did too. In the summers he'd ride every day, both ways just to chat it up, often giving impromptu sermons to fellow riders who were willing to listen. Many were willing. It was his big smile and even bigger personality. For him, a Christian life didn't mean sainthood. It meant living a good, honest life and giving to others. His sermons weren't about the Gospel as much as they were about how a life should be lived and enjoyed. Biblical lessons from thousands of years ago are still a solid outline, but today's sinner needed forgiveness, understanding and more than anything, a second chance.

As Pastor Isakson turned from Howard Street onto Second Avenue, he paused for a brief moment and wondered if he had time to run into the McDonald's across the street and grab a burger. But he was already five minutes late and if he left the kids up to their own devices, Lord knows what trouble they'd get into.

He mounted the steps to the main entrance of St. Mark's, but something else caught his eye—what looked like a homeless man sleeping on the sidewalk.

The police hadn't been very lenient about the homeless lying about around his church. They said that the sidewalks were meant for walking, not sleeping and the bums needed to move along. Since those "bums" were the majority of his congregation, he didn't like them being harassed. But more so, he didn't want them out in this cold. The church's homeless shelter had closed years ago, but he could always find a warm place inside for a willing Christian.

So before entering the church, he woke up the sleeping man.

***

Edwin's head was pounding and he was wet from head to toe. He slowly glanced around without sitting up and realized that he was sprawled out on a wooden bench. Not a bench, a church pew. He tried to raise his head, but saw dancing spots and thought better of it. He closed his eyes and tried to make it go away. His stomach lurched and he rolled onto his side. A white bucket sat on the floor below his head. He vomited into it until nothing else would come up.

"I thought he was a member of our church," a man said from somewhere nearby. "When I invited him inside to warm up, I realized we'd never met. I let him in anyway though. That's just what we do here."

"I'm glad you called, he didn't come back to his store today. I was getting a bit worried about him myself," a woman said.

It was Amelia. Edwin hadn't known her long but her voice was unmistakable. It always sounded singsong happy and Edwin couldn't figure out why.

"You said he has a store?" Pastor Isakson asked.

"Yes. He owns Mr. Z's, the toy store. Do you know it?"

"Oh, yes. Of course," he said, looking away. "I knew the family. Such a tragedy."

"I'm sorry? But I'm not sure what—"

A teenage girl interrupted them.

"Pastor Isakson," she said in an annoyed tone. "We've been waitin' for you for a while now. Are we going to practice tonight or should I send them all home?"

"Nellie, what did we talk about?" Pastor Isakson said calmly. "When you need to speak with an adult who is already engaged in conversation, you need to say, 'excuse me' before you begin. It's only polite."

"Excuse me," she said, "but we're going to leave if you aren't going to do the rehearsal. So let's move it."

Pastor Isakson sighed.

"Very well then."

Amelia watched as Pastor Isakson and the girl walked to the stage where a group of 20 or so kids sat waiting. He began directing the kids to their assigned places on the stage.

The lights were dimmed which helped ease Edwin's pounding head. He managed to sit up and take in his surroundings. It looked vaguely familiar, but he couldn't place why. The center stage was a biblical manger scene with a straw crib for baby Jesus. The kids stood around taking turns as wise men or carrying masks that identified them as animals. The donkey and chicken masks were obvious from the back of the church, but the rest were a bit obscure. They were hand-drawn, probably by the kids themselves.

Amelia sat down next to Edwin as the rehearsal began.

The wise men tripped over their long robes, while the donkey and the chicken danced behind them. A rather irate Joseph, shouted at the innkeeper about obtaining a room, this time not taking no for an answer. It nearly came to blows, which wasn't how Edwin remembered it, but he was still pretty drunk.

Pastor Isakson halted the rehearsal when a boy swiped the baby Jesus from the crib and began tossing the doll to another boy like a football.

"It's going to be quite a show," Amelia said.

"A complete disaster," Edwin said.

"Not at all. Look at their faces," she said. "They're just having a good time. And they're here, that's what matters. The enthusiasm is obvious. They just need a little coaching."

"Or a probation officer."

Amelia put her left hand on Edwin's cheek and felt the day's worth of stubble. She turned his face to look at her own and saw the blue eyes that she remembered from the first day they'd met. Sure, they were bloodshot, but the rich blue was still there.

"Are you really this guy?" she asked, her voice soft. "The guy who skips out on work, gets drunk and barfs in a church? Because I'm starting to wonder if the man who drove my son home—my new employer, mind you—is the man I thought he was a few days ago."

"I didn't ask to hire you and I didn't ask you to come here," Edwin said, pulling away and looking at the floor.

"No, some stranger called me," she was frustrated and angry with Edwin. "This stranger said he found my number in some man's pocket and that I needed to come get you."

"I would have been fine. Who needs you? Leave me alone."

As Edwin said it he tried to convince himself it was the truth, but he couldn't.

He did need someone. His soaked clothes and vomit bucket told him that. He was in a dark place and as much as he'd like to hide it, he was glad Amelia was sitting next to him, even in his sorry state.

"OK then, I'll leave you alone," she said. She stood to leave, but Edwin took her hand.

"Wait. I'm sorry. It's just, that I don't know how to do this."

"Do what exactly?"

"This—talk to someone—you know."

"You just talk. Then listen."

"I haven't talked—I mean really talked to somebody in a long time," he said, still looking at the floor. "Everything's gone to crap. It's over. There's nothing else to say."

"You mean the store? Businesses fail all the time. You can't keep your self-worth wrapped up in something like that. You did your best. Now it's time for something new. I'm sure you can find something else."

"It's not that easy. I can't let it fail. It's not mine to let go."

"I don't understand. I thought you owned the store."

"I do, but I didn't start it. Seriously, it's been open for like 40 years, did you think I started it from the womb?"

"I thought that you bought it," she said.

"I inherited it."

"From your family?"

"From my wife."

Twelve

Eleven months earlier

Spokane International Airport is divided into three concourses—A, B and C. For a regional airport, it's big enough to get people where they need to go, but since the airport hadn't done any major remodeling since the 9/11 security changes, there was nothing to do at the airport for people waiting for their loved ones to arrive. All the good stuff—including the coffee place—was on the other side of the security gate. Empty tile-floored corridors filled with fluorescent lights welcomed the waiting. Edwin watched the snow outside and the headlights of cars as they drove by.

Edwin paced back and forth holding a bouquet of flowers near the exit of Concourse C's security lines. The airport was nearly shut down. Even on a busy holiday travel weekend, flights didn't come into or go out of Spokane after 11 p.m. It was now close to midnight and the only people left standing around were all waiting for the same flight: Alaska Airlines Flight 23 from Seattle which had yet to arrive and people were starting to wonder why.

Edwin looked through the security gate, punishing himself by looking for the coffee place, which he knew wasn't open anyway. If he didn't get some caffeine in him soon, he was likely to drop on the spot.

He was exhausted.

With the holiday rush at Mr. Z's, he'd been working 14 hours a day just to get by. He hadn't even had the time to get out the Christmas decorations Mary loved so much. There was just so much to do and he'd never had to do it all alone before.

He feared the tongue-lashing he'd get from Mary for not decorating the store for Christmas, but he thought she'd understand once she saw how hard he'd been working to keep the store afloat.

He suppressed a yawn. He hadn't seen Mary in four months and he didn't want her first impression of him to be of a tired, worn-down man who was barely keeping it together. She deserved better.

Flight 23 was supposed to land 45 minutes ago. The digital Arrivals sign still read "On Time." Edwin marveled at how the time kept by normal people differed from airline time.

An elderly woman in a white knit cap, who was waiting for the same flight had already picked up the courtesy phone and inquired about the plane's arrival, but they told her they had no information other than it was listed as "On Time" and should be arriving any moment.

"It's only a 50 minute flight," she said as she took a seat next to Edwin. He'd finally stopped pacing. "They don't know squat. I should have just told my son to find his own way home. I'd be in bed right now."

Edwin nodded to the woman, but wasn't really listening. He was thinking back to years ago when the Spokane airport allowed anyone through security. You used to be able to walk right up to an arrival gate and meet the passengers—no boarding passes or ID checks required.

In college Mary and Edwin were broke. They couldn't even afford a night at the movies, but they loved to people-watch. And the airport had the best free people-watching around. They would spend hours watching the people waiting to depart—guessing where they might be going and making up wild stories about the things they would do when they got there.

"She's off to meet her lover in Dallas," Mary had said once, looking a woman sitting alone reading a USA Today.

"How do you figure?" Edwin had said.

"It's the boots. Snake skin. And she just took off her wedding ring."

"Good eye, but you failed to mention one other thing."

"And what's that?"

"Her lover is a rodeo clown with a second family in Austin."

"And where did that discovery come from?"

"No idea, but it sounds better," Edwin had said.

Mary had smiled and snuggled just a little bit closer to Edwin.

"Agreed."

Nearly every weekend they would set off for the airport just to watch. Sure, the people-watching was great, but it was also time they had to themselves. No studying. No working. No dishes or house cleaning. And it wasn't like they never saw each other. Edwin would visit her at the store every day during his lunch break from his job at a used car lot. They saw each other every night at their apartment too, but by then they were both beat. Mary was tired from her classes in the morning and working with her father at the store at night. Edwin's classes came easy to him, but the grind at the car lot was enough to tire anyone. So the airport time—time to themselves—was special.

But today as Edwin looked around the corridor, his mind couldn't make up tall tales about those waiting with him. Their faces were too drawn. Too worried. He too was worried. The plane should have been here by now. *Where was it?*

From the other side of the corridor there was a commotion as some one in a suit came out from an office door. Standing behind him were two airport police officers.

A woman approached the men, screamed and fell to her knees.

The old lady in the knit cap next to Edwin sucked in a breathy sob and covered her mouth with her hand. Edwin helped her up by the elbow.

"Come on, let's go see what this is all about," he said.

The walk was in slow motion, not because the elderly woman's pace was lagging, but because Edwin knew that when he heard what the man in the suit had to say, that it would be real. Something happened to the plane. Whatever was wrong would be reality and there was no turning back.

Edwin and the woman stood in front of the man in the suit. His hair was gray and matted, as if he had just woken up. His eyes were moist and narrowed.

"There was an accident," he said with great effort. "The plane. It went down somewhere over the Cascades. There were no survivors we know of."

"My boy!" the elderly woman said, falling into Edwin's arms crying. Her weight, little as it was, hit Edwin like a ton of bricks. He slowly sunk to the ground clutching her around the shoulders. He held her tight because it just seemed like the right thing to do.

Maybe it was just a story, Edwin thought. Maybe Mary never made it on the flight. She had to make a connection or two after all. The airlines probably put her up in a hotel somewhere like Salt Lake City or Chicago. These people were all mourning loved ones, but he wasn't like them. He couldn't be. Edwin reached for his phone to check his messages. Certainly she would have called and told him not to come to the airport.

He fumbled with the phone, his hands shaking so badly that it squirted out of his hands and onto the tile floor. The shiny surface allowed the phone to slide a few feet, stopping only when it hit some man's black boots. Army boots. Edwin looked up to see a large man in a camouflage uniform with a black cross on his chest.

"Edwin Klein? Husband of Mary Klein?" he said, but the words didn't register.

Mary was gone.

Edwin stared at the snow outside and the blinding headlights of the passing cars. His world was torn apart.

Thirteen

Present Day
Seattle, Washington

Lance Massey stared at the newspaper website open in front of him. The glare from the Seattle skyline behind him reflected on the screen. The 45th floor of the Evergreen Building had million dollar views. To be more precise, his was a $10 million view, roughly the combined value of the 12 floors in the building he owned and leased to various tech companies that prized a view of the Space Needle, Mt. Rainier and the Puget Sound. The 55-year-old wasn't too fond of the kids who worked on the floors near his corporate offices. They were too loud for his tastes, but their money was just as green as the next guy's.

He had made a fortune buying up old buildings up and down the West Coast and converting them into hip, modern spaces for maximum profit. For the Evergreen Building project he had to take on investors, but he had managed to keep the title to some of the best floors. He smiled thinking of how he suckered his investors into forfeiting their claims to the floors. They sued him, but lost. He knew the benefits of never getting emotional about battles over his developments. It was all business, which allowed him to operate in a cold, detached manner. His competitors nicknamed him Mr. Ice. He liked it so much that he had it engraved on his office door. He was the man and nobody stood in his way when he wanted something. Nobody.

But today his focus wasn't on his Seattle properties, but rather on a project he was working on in Spokane.

He read through the short story from a Spokane news website. The headline read, "Pipe Causes Flood at Downtown Building." The story gave sparse details of the event. A pipe had cracked, flooded the building and then froze after streaming out onto the sidewalk. Pretty uneventful.

Massey thought it unlikely the reporter had even called Mr. Z's to get a full account of what transpired. But the reporter had included one detail that was of particular interest to him. The store was planning to be closed for a few days during repairs, but would reopen. They hired some help to get the job done quickly.

He frowned at the news. He had hoped to have this Mr. Z's fiasco wrapped up before his annual holiday trip to Hawaii, but this little bug of a man—Edwin Klein—was threatening to destroy the entire deal. Never before had a helpless building owner held on for so long. He'd already made two offers, one at market value, then one slightly below market value. He figured that if he had upped his offer, he'd look like he was desperate for the property and all the leverage would be in the seller's hands. By low-balling him, he showed interest, but didn't tip his hand. Either way Klein had turned him down twice and Lance Massey didn't like it one bit.

The soft approach wasn't working. He'd have to double up his efforts.

He pulled out the designer's rendering of Riverside Avenue. A luxury hotel anchored one corner, while a collection of restaurants and retail stores, all connected by an inviting center garden filled the rest of the block. He'd secured every other piece of property on the block, buying them through dummy corporations so word wouldn't get out that the land was hot. He knew that going against the grain was the best strategy—buy when few are buying. In the down economy building owners were much more willing to sell—most of them at least.

The tenants of the buildings didn't know their days were numbered. Soon a wrecking ball would level the entire block to make way for his project. His original plan included saving some of the buildings, including Mr. Z's, but when he showed the plans to prospective hotel chains, he was rebuffed. They wanted more space and were willing to pay for it. He just needed to get each building under his control.

But Massey had one hold out—a little good-for-nothing toy store. It was time to turn up the heat.

He pushed a button on this desk phone, summoning his assistant.

"Caroline, book me on the next flight to Spokane," he said. "I need to pick up a few things for Christmas."

Fourteen

Spokane

"Tell me about Mary," Amelia said, handing Edwin a cup of coffee. The morning light was just hitting the living room through the blustery snow outside.

"I don't know . . ." Edwin said, accepting the cup with a weak hand.

Amelia had spent the night on the couch at Edwin's house. They couldn't find his car the night before, so she drove him home. Not that he was in any condition to drive anyhow. But the roads were so bad that she feared trying to get back to her apartment across town alone. A neighbor woman back at the apartment was watching the kids and agreed to keep them overnight—just this one time. She hated to ask, but it was better than having her car run off the road.

She should not have stayed the night at Edwin's house. For all she knew he was a psycho killer or could have attacked her during some crazy night terror. But for some reason it was OK. There was something about Edwin, even sloppy drunk Edwin, that Amelia was comfortable with. It wasn't an attraction, although he was a handsome man.

Maybe it was just curiosity. Edwin was raw and hurting. He wore his emotions on his sleeve, unlike Josh who hid his feelings. She had to compare every man she met to Josh, because that's all she knew.

Edwin was obviously embarrassed about the whole situation, but didn't argue when she told him she planned on staying the night. He had moved some piles of clothes off the couch for her and then went into his own room and didn't come out until the morning. Apparently he wasn't a psycho killer after all.

She identified with Edwin, but she couldn't put her finger on why. Maybe it was the way that, even through his brooding, she could see that he was a kind man, gentle even. He owned his own business. True, it was in tatters, but Josh couldn't boast anything close to having business acumen. That made a difference to her.

Edwin had sadness in his eyes. It was the same sadness that she saw in her sister's eyes when their mother died of a drug overdose. She, just like Edwin, looked empty and devoid of all desire for consolation. He was heartbroken. But Amelia sensed that Edwin wasn't destined to be alone, regardless of not putting up much of a fight to keep his life in order either.

The drinking was certainly a problem, but she'd been around enough drunks to know how to navigate those dark and choppy waters. He wasn't a textbook drunk, at least not yet.

He seemed to be using the booze to hide his pain, but disliked his own actions. When she called him on it last night, she felt like a teacher scolding a schoolboy. He was sheepish and said he knew he needed to cool it.

He was punishing himself, it was clear. He was trying to put himself in a bad place through the drinking. It wasn't an escape for him though.

It was a sentence. A punishment.

It wasn't until last night, when he told her about Mary, that she understood the source of his pain. But she didn't know the whole story and now she was extremely curious.

"I think it'll do you good to talk about her," she said. "You're obviously in love with her. Tell me your story."

"I'm not real big on sharing," he said.

"Tell me something I don't know," she said, not hiding the sarcasm. "Have you talked to anyone about her since she passed?"

Edwin said nothing, but shook his head no. He wrapped his hands around his cup of coffee and let the steam rise up into his face. He sat for a long moment, not saying anything. Amelia just assumed he'd passed on the opportunity to talk, but then he began to speak. And when he talked about Mary, his eyes lit up.

"We met in high school," he said. "She was a freshman and I was a senior. There was this terrible ice storm that hit Spokane. Half the city lost power when tree branches and ice snapped power lines. The school lost power too, right in the middle of class, so they released us to go home. I had a four-wheel drive truck, so I gave a few of my friends a ride home. Somehow Mary managed to get her way into the pick-up. She told me later that she'd been waiting for an opportunity to bump into me and the ice storm seemed like the perfect chance."

"So you started dating after that?"

"No, not at all," he said. "I can say it now, but didn't recognize it then. I was a typical upper classman. I didn't give much thought to freshmen. And to be honest I don't really remember much about giving Mary a ride home either. She was just some girl."

He took another sip of coffee and continued.

"After that day I didn't speak to her for months," he said.

"Hold on a minute," Amelia said. "I thought this was a love story?"

"I'm getting there," he said. "We were just kids, remember?"

"Just checking."

"We didn't talk again until later that winter," Edwin recalled. "There was this Sadie Hawkins dance. You know, the one where the girl asks the guy to the dance? I expected to go, but nobody had asked me. I didn't give it much thought until Mary cornered me in the cafeteria and asked me to go. She had this sun-streaked blonde hair, pulled back by a clip. She looked like she'd just come back from the beach, which was impossible since it was still cold outside. Her face was full of color. She reminded me of summer. She was beautiful."

"So you took her to the dance."

"Yes. I picked her up at Mr. Z's where she was working with her parents. That's when I realized that the "Z" was for Zimmerman. I'd been to the store before, but never met the owners. Her dad grilled me about where we were going, how we'd get there and when she'd be back home. I thought it was a casual date, but it was serious business for them."

"I can understand that as a parent."

"The dance was terrible. A fight broke out in the middle of the dance floor and they sent everybody home when the police showed up. We ended up getting burgers and milkshakes at this hamburger stand downtown called Dick's. It's been around forever. We sat in the cab of the pick-up truck in the parking lot and just talked for hours. She told me about her family's trip to Mexico, which was the reason she was so tan."

"That makes sense."

"We just clicked. I don't know how to explain it. I know that kids in high school aren't supposed to be in love. Everyone is too immature and inexperienced to know what it all means, but that's all I ever knew. I knew I wanted to be with her and she wanted to be with me. That's all we needed."

"I think that's all anyone ever needs. Even at that age. Even today."

"We were together through college. Well, I was in college off and on, while she finished up high school. We moved in together when she graduated, then got married six months later."

"It sounds like you two were meant to be."

"She's the only woman I've ever loved."

"You decided not to have any children?"

"We tried, believe me, we tried," he said. "She became pregnant, but miscarried at three months."

"I'm so sorry," Amelia said.

"It was a little girl," he said. "Mary never got pregnant again. We saw doctors to figure out why it wasn't happening. She took it pretty hard when they finally said she wouldn't be able to have any kids. Something internally wouldn't allow it. She was so good with kids in the toy store, it was tough for her, knowing that she couldn't have any of her own. But I didn't care. We had each other and that's all that mattered to me."

"That's a lot for a couple to go through," she said.

They sat in silence for a while and Amelia noticed that tears had welled up in Edwin's eyes. For a guy that wasn't big on sharing, he'd just unloaded a lot that had been held deep inside. Edwin quickly wiped the tears away with his shirtsleeve, pretending to be looking at his watch.

"The store is the only thing I have left of hers," he said.

"That's not true and you know it," she said. "The feelings you felt. The feelings you feel today for her are real, even if she's gone. What's the store got to do with it?"

"She wanted it to be successful, to be like it always was. That's the only reason she signed up with the Army National Guard. To keep the store afloat."

"But she didn't want you miserable either," Amelia said. "You can't forget that."

"That doesn't matter to me. I've got to make it work. It will work. I know it," he said. Talking about Mary had helped him clear his head. He knew what needed to be done. "Now, I need to get into the store before it gets too late this morning. We need to reopen tomorrow."

"The floors are ready, we should be all set. Maybe we can open today?"

"There's one thing I've been avoiding for too long that needs to be done before we can open for real. Are your kids available to help today?"

"I guess, but they probably can't help too much," she said. "What do you have in mind?"

"Mr. Z's needs a slight makeover."

Fifteen

Lance Massey stepped out of the warm airport to hail a cab to downtown Spokane and quickly remembered that hailing a cab in Spokane was a fool's errand. There just weren't any around. Stupid hick town, he thought. He'd traveled the country developing properties, but there was something about Spokane that didn't sit well with him. To him, Spokane was the red-headed stepchild of the West side of the state. The powerful people came from the Puget Sound, not Eastern Washington. He questioned himself for even trying to develop a project here, but there was a profit to be made and he'd come too far along in this process to let it slip away now.

He forgot the cab altogether and decided to rent a car from the only car rental counter that was still open. He got the cheapest car they had, a little four-door coupe that was probably not the wisest choice, given the snow. His regular rental agency wasn't open and the little twerp behind the counter in his red polo and teenage soul patch of chin hairs wasn't going to extend him an upgrade-courtesy to something practical.

Massey was a brute who expected anyone in his way to simply fold and do his bidding. He was used to getting his way and didn't like being told no. When challenged he would lash out. His assistant was terrified of the man, preferring to get her instructions over the intercom system, which was a safe distance away. Massey was proud that his employees avoided him.

He once famously drove a pick-up truck into the side of an under-construction office building extension to tell his superintendent that the man had placed the doorway on the wrong side. No one was surprised. His ridiculous antics were expected. Thus people did as they were told to avoid the embarrassment of a Mass-Meltdown, as his tirades were known.

Massey's ill temper was on full display at the rental counter. The kid practically threw the keys at him in protest. Massey returned the favor with a grunt and a stern lecture about the customer always being right. He was certain it fell on deaf-and-dumb ears. Most people didn't understand him or how he operated, but he preferred it that way. It kept people on their toes.

When he stepped outside to find the car, he was blasted by the snow and bitter cold. Massey didn't mind Seattle's rain, but he despised the snow. The car was parked in row 11, space 26, which just happened to be the last row and space in the entire lot. By the time he reached the car, his Salvatore Ferragamo Python Loafers were soaked through to his socks and his expression had gone even more sour.

The car was iced over, so much so that he had to scrape the handle with the edge of his American Express card just to get the door open. He got inside, started the engine and cranked the heat. He tried the windshield wipers to clear his view, but when he flipped the switch nothing happened. Upon inspection he discovered they were frozen to the windshield. The car wasn't in a covered area—like the dozens of similar cars he passed walking to this one. The rental kid gave me this car on purpose, he thought. He exited the car and began peeling the frozen wipers off the windshield.

Maybe renting a car wasn't such a good idea. As he considered returning the keys, a blue SUV flew by him in the parking lot, splashing him with a puddle of slush. He looked back to the rental car building. Maybe he could change in there. But all the lights were turned off. Everyone had already gone home.

The SUV skidded around 180 degrees and returned in Massey's direction. He jumped back into the car determined not to get splashed again. As the SUV roared passed him, the rental car kid, in his red polo shirt, rolled down his window and flipped him the bird.

Massey really hated Spokane.

Sixteen

Little 6-year-old Susanna wasn't a great deal of help decorating the store for Christmas, but she was more than happy to be a "toy tester," playing alone in front of the register. Edwin was pleased the toys were at least getting some use, not just sitting on a shelf, never to be purchased by anyone. The store was finally taking on the holiday charm that Edwin remembered. A lot of that charm came from the sounds emanating from the little girl and that made him feel good.

The store was perfect for holiday decorations. The main floor was filled with rich, dark wood shelving units with small hooks and buttons that were hidden under the top shelf to hang all sorts of decorations. The second-floor balcony wrapped around the South and East walls of the store. A carved railing overlooked the entire store and the street outside. The building had housed a number of businesses since the early 1900s. One of the framed photographs on the wall showed B. Smith's Drug Store, which had leased the space in the 1920s. After that it was an accounting business and a fabric store. The rich history was never lost on Edwin or his customers.

Amelia took charge of the decorations, directing Edwin and her 11-year-old son Marcus where to place each item.

"It needs to go higher than that," Amelia said to Marcus, who was standing dangerously close to the top of a ladder, hanging a large yellow star from a ceiling rafter.

"It can't go any higher, mom," Marcus said in disgust. "I can't hang it on the ceiling."

"Just move it to the right a little. It looks like there is already a hook you can attach it to."

"And you expect my arms to grow a foot?"

"No. I expect you to climb down and move the ladder over. And curb the attitude, mister. Remember, you're still working off your debt."

"Fine, Mom."

Despite his protests, Marcus was a good worker who seemed to derive some sense of joy in getting a rise out of his mom, which he tried to do at every turn. He did as he was told, but was sure to let everyone know he wasn't too happy about it.

"You know, Marcus," Edwin said. "A little old lady used to hang that star, with no complaints at all."

"Maybe you should have asked her to do it, then," he said.

"Marcus!" Amelia said. "That's enough!"

"It's alright," Edwin said, in Amelia's direction. "He didn't know."

Edwin turned to Marcus.

"The couple that used to own this store, Mr. and Mrs. Zimmerman were well-known in the city for their holiday decorations throughout the store and in the front display windows. But they've both passed on now. So it's up to us to carry on the tradition."

"Sorry, man, I didn't know," Marcus said, repositioning the ladder to hang the garland.

"No problem," Edwin said. "You're doing a great job and I appreciate it."

Marcus' emotions got the best of him and he beamed after getting a compliment from someone who wasn't his mother. He wasn't used to being around men except for his dad, but he hadn't seen him in months.

Marcus took note of how his mom looked at Edwin. It was the same way she used to look at his dad before he left.

Marcus thought Edwin was OK, even if he did bust him for shoplifting. He wondered what it would be like to have Edwin around more, like his dad used to be. It was lonely with just his mom and sister. He missed his aunt and cousins in Bonners Ferry too. He used to played sports with his cousin Max every weekend. He was particularly interested in hockey and knew how to ice skate a little, but when he mentioned it to his mom, she seemed confused and changed the subject. Marcus figured that she just didn't know that much about sports.

"Edwin, do you know anything about hockey?" Marcus asked, still on top of the ladder.

"A little, I guess," Edwin said. "I never played, but I like to go to the Chiefs games."

"What's that?"

"Spokane's team. The Chiefs."

"There's a hockey team here?" Marcus asked with obvious enthusiasm. "Mom, why didn't you tell me?"

Amelia shrugged her shoulders, signaling she had no idea what they were talking about in the first place.

"Do you think we could go to a game?" Marcus asked Edwin.

Edwin caught Amelia's eye and without saying anything she seemed to indicate that it would be OK for him to take her son to a game.

"Yeah, I think we could work something out."

"Awesome!" Marcus said.

"But first we need to finish up the decorating for tomorrow's opening," Edwin said. "There are a bunch of boxes left in the backroom labeled 'Windows.' Can you start moving them to the display windows in front?"

Marcus didn't reply. In an instant he was off to move the boxes.

"I hope that was OK," Amelia said, when Marcus was out of sight "He doesn't have a lot of male role models. He gets kind of excited."

"It'll be fun. Just the guys," but even as he said it, he started to question the offer.

Amelia smiled, knowing how much a hockey game would mean to her son, but at the same time, wondering if Edwin was the role model she wanted for her Marcus. She'd already seen him at his worst, or darn close to it, and they barely knew each other. Yet, as she went about the business of decorating the rest of the store she started to see the Edwin that Mary must have seen— happy, kind and strong. He'd stop between his own tasks and play with Susanna, making her giggle with funny faces or by voicing the stuffed animals she was playing with. He and Marcus were talking too, and her son's poor attitude wasn't the reason. They were actually enjoying each other's company. It was wonderful to see.

She was a bit sad when all of the decorations had been placed, knowing the day would be coming to an end. The entire store seemed to be covered in green, silver, gold and red decorations that sparkled with hints of twinkle lights and gold bells. A sprinkling of yellow stars hung from the walls and ceiling, leaving a fairy-tale impression. The decor was certainly over-the-top, but what Christmas display wasn't? The only thing left to do was decorate the display windows, but Edwin had already told her that he planned to do the windows by himself that night. He wanted to save that particular job for himself.

Amelia, knowing Edwin wanted to be alone, packed up the kids and told him she'd see him in the morning.

* * *

Through the front display windows Edwin watched Amelia and the kids walk to their car. Before him sat a series of brown cardboard boxes, all labeled "Windows." Mary had meticulously labeled each box with a number using a purple pen. The display windows were her project and he was just the messenger to make it happen. He knew once he opened box number one that he'd have the details he needed to decorate the full scene inside the window. But something was holding him back. He stood with the boxes for a long time, just waiting—postponing the task before him.

When he finally found the courage to reach down and touch the box, he simply couldn't make his hands open it. He placed his palms flat on the surface of the box—Mary's box—and felt himself collapse to his knees. Kneeling on the floor of the dimly lit toy store, illuminated by a smattering of Christmas lights, Edwin wept aloud. It was the suppressed tears of a man who had lost his love. His everything. He was sitting in her store, looking at her handwriting on the outside of the box. He couldn't take his hands off the box. They were the final things he would ever receive from her and he didn't want to let them go.

Once he opened the boxes, he'd never again be with his wife. Although it seemed silly to characterize it that way. Somehow keeping the decorations inside the boxes kept those memories alive. He could smell the perfume she must have been wearing the night before she shipped out to her National Guard training in Texas. It was the same night she packed the boxes. Sure, they had talked and video-chatted many times after, but that night he had held her close for the last time. And she held him too. They spent a passionate night together, not saying a word.

Did she know it would be the last time?

No. Edwin couldn't bare the thought. But there was something different about that night. They just couldn't talk the way they usually talked. They were off. She seemed distant and he was nervous for her. He didn't see it at the time, but looking back on it now, he could see that she was hurting. Scared. She didn't want to leave, but she'd made a decision and would stick with it. Damn the reality of it all.

It wasn't supposed to be her joining the National Guard. It was his idea to sign up and he was ready for the task ahead of him. Had he not failed the physical because of his heart condition, Mary would still be alive. He could imagine Mary sitting alone in the toy store without him. She wouldn't have been a miserable wreck like him. She was stronger. Stronger than any person he'd ever known. But he was weak and lost without her.

He could still imagine her when he closed his eyes. The video of their lives together played on an endless loop in his head. He could see her face and touch her skin. She would always come back to him in his dreams. But that's all they are now. Dreams. They were wonderful dreams that contrasted too much with the stark reality of his life. The failing store, the alcohol and now the entrance of this other woman in his life. Amelia. He wondered what Mary would think of him spending time with another woman. She'd hate it, he thought, but the comparison wasn't fair. The Mary he knew was his loving wife—his partner. Of course she wouldn't want him to be with someone else. But that Mary wasn't reality anymore. She's just a memory and it's not fair. Not fair to Mary. Not fair to him.

He wrestled with these thoughts for a long time, recognizing that his internal struggles were helping him avoid the one task he knew he had to accomplish tonight. Follow Mary's instructions and decorate the windows.

On that last morning when Mary left, she told him to be sure and move the window decoration boxes to the store's backroom and hold onto them until two weeks after Halloween before opening them. The instructions inside would tell him everything he needed to know.

It was time.

He blew the dust off the top of box number one and pealed back the packing tape that held it closed. He folded back the lid and peered inside. Laying atop a pile of faux bricks for a chimney were two envelopes. The first was a large manila envelope with the word "Instructions" written on it. He set it to the side.

The second envelope was smaller and gold colored. Printed on the envelope in Mary's neat cursive handwriting were three words.

"For My Eddie."

Seventeen

Edwin turned the envelope over in his hands. It was thin and sealed up tight. His heart jumped into his throat and he could hear the blood pumping in his ears. He hadn't expected to find a message for him. With all the high-hopes of a giddy teenager, he tore open the envelope and pulled out its contents—two pieces of folded notebook paper. The edges were shredded from being pulled away from a spiral-bound notebook. He tried to read the words, but the lighting inside the store was too dim. Rather than simply turn on a light across the room, he stepped up into the display window and sat on a wooden crate. The bright streetlights were enough to illuminate the pages. His back was to the interior of the store, so anyone walking by would see him clearly with his elbows resting on his knees. But he shut that world out and began to read. Soon tears poured down his face.

* * *

Dear Eddie,

I miss you and I haven't even left yet. I guess that's been the hardest part of this new chapter in our lives—being away from you. I knew what I was in for with the National Guard, but I tried to ignore it and as I sit here writing this I wish we'd done something else. But deep in my heart I know it's the right thing because this job and the bonus will save the store, at least for a little while.

I can't say this out loud like I should, but I want to apologize to you too. When I took your place with the Guard, I was only thinking of me. Could I do that job?

Could I be a soldier like you had intended to be? What I ignored was you. Could you do what I was going to do? Would you want to be alone at the toy store, with its problems and never-ending stream of decisions? Obviously you could because you're wonderful, but would you want to? I never asked. So as I pack my bag to leave tomorrow, I'm still afraid to ask you that. What if you said no? I don't know where that would leave us.

This store is my family. I grew up here and spent more time walking down its aisles than I ever spent at a dinner table with my parents. It's all I've ever known and what I identify with. I guess that's why I want it to work for us. I want that family—my version of family, as weird as that sounds. I'm not sure how else to do it. But again, I never asked you. It was all about me.

You are the best man I've ever known. You've stood by me, regardless of the obstacles before us, and never wavered. This is what makes us strong. You make us strong. Strong forever.

I owe you more than I can ever attempt to repay, but that doesn't mean I can't try. When I get back lets talk about the horse stables again. I've got some ideas that might get us where we need to be. I know that you have always wanted to own a stable and to share what you know about riding with children. I shouldn't put my dreams before yours. Your dreams are mine too. I see that now.

You'll find this out soon enough, but you've already walked in to the dining room twice and interrupted me while I'm writing this letter. You're a lovable pest, for sure.

Thank you for being you. I love you and always will. I want you to be happy and I want to spend the rest of my life making that happen, no matter what. I'll see you soon.

Love always, *Mary*

* * *

Edwin read the letter again and again. Questioning, but at the same time cherishing every word and tear. Why did she write this letter? Why didn't she just tell him how she felt? They had the sort of relationship that they could share these things. If he could have talked with her, he could have reassured her that he was OK with their decisions. But now it was too late.

She'd mentioned the horse stables. She'd brought it up a few times in the past, but he was always the one to shoot it down. The stable and ranch were a luxury that they couldn't afford. Sure, it's where he felt the most comfortable, but it wasn't financially feasible to just start up a stable. People just didn't do that. Especially when their small business was failing. But she was still thinking about his needs and that made Edwin hurt and feel the pain of losing her even more.

He cursed himself for not having the courage to open the boxes of decorations sooner. He'd kept her final words locked up for over a year because he was afraid. What a coward. He was so focused on reading the pages, that he didn't notice the man watching him from across the street.

* * *

Edwin wiped away the tears that had streaked his face. He was still sitting in the store's window, now fully aware that he was on display for the dozens if not hundreds of people who were out and about downtown that night. Even on a snowy weeknight, the sidewalks were filled. A few potential customers even came to the front door, tried the handle, then finally read the sign that said, "Merry Christmas. Closed for Repairs. To Reopen Dec. 21."

Part of Edwin thought he should just let them in. If they wanted to shop amongst the chaos of the store's repairs and holiday decorating, then so be it. But he knew that wasn't the image customers should have of Mr. Z's. He couldn't offer the lowest prices or best selection, but he could offer charm. A cluttered mess wasn't charming at all.

Edwin put Mary's letter into his pants pocket, not wanting to set it down where it might get misplaced. He then opened the envelope marked "Instructions" and sat back down on the crate in despair. Mary's window scene wasn't the scene she'd promised him. It was more personal than a bland Christmas village. This project was going to take all night. He'd be lucky to finish by morning. He made a pot of coffee and got to work.

Eighteen

Lance Massey sat at Snyder's Steakhouse slowly eating a prime rib dinner. His cloth napkin was folded neatly across his lap. He only removed it to dab drips off his chin. He savored the flavor of each pricey bite. His waitress was an unsurprising dolt of a server who was unlikely to receive any tip at all. The only positive thing he could say about his dinner experience concerned the view and the pathetic one-man show he was watching from across the street. From the second-floor window seat he'd reserved the day before, he had a wonderful view of his future hotel and retail development. The constant stream of patrons walking past made him furious. He was furious because his development wasn't built and with every passerby, he was missing out on a customer and it was costing him money.

There was only one thing in his way—that ridiculous Mr. Z's toy store.

Massey couldn't keep his eyes off of Edwin Klein, who had been sitting in the front window for nearly an hour. He thought he might be reading a book, but he just held a few papers in his hand. By the time Massey's terrible waitress finally offered coffee and a desert menu, Edwin had started unpacking boxes in the window.

He worked methodically from box to box. Massey figured the window box had to be about 12 feet high and roughly 25 feet wide with wooden panes crisscrossing the span. The window box was deep. Wasted retail space, Massey thought.

Edwin first hung eight long strips of alternating red and green fabric on hooks at the top of the window box, near the back, setting a backdrop for the scene. He left two strips rolled up high so he could enter and exit the window. He attached items to the sidewalls, slowly constructing a realistic looking chimney, complete with a hearth and mantel. He filled the mantel with an assortment of decorations, then finally hung stockings from the base.

Two Christmas trees were set up in just moments. One tree had lights and decorations already on it. Edwin just had to piece it together and plug it in. Massey wondered why the scene, obviously a living room, would have two Christmas trees. One was tall, its star reaching the height of the window box. Other than the star, it was bare—no decorations or lights whatsoever. Yet the other tree that just reached the man's waist was lit up like a Fourth of July fireworks display.

Massey's family had never put up a tree during Christmas and thus, he didn't put one up today at his own home. His parents thought the hassle of the holiday was best spent on other pursuits and Massey agreed wholeheartedly. What was the point? Sure, the economic stimulation caused by eggnog drinkers racking up credit card debt was a benefit to the bottom line, but what gain was it to them? The gift of giving? What a load of bull.

The restaurant was nearly empty when Massey decided he'd had enough watching. He hadn't come all this way to just watch Edwin Klein. It was time for them to talk man-to-man.

* * *

"There's something special about watching another man work," came the voice from behind Edwin.

"You can't be in here," Edwin said, not able to see the man who had somehow gotten into his store. He was standing behind the cloth panels. "Get out."

"Then you should have locked the door, Edwin," Massey said.

Edwin recognized the voice now. It was Lance Massey, the man who had twice previously offered to buy the Mr. Z's building. Edwin climbed out of the window box.

"I don't know what makes you think you can just walk in here like you own the place," Edwin said in disgust.

"That's just it. I don't own the place," Massey said. "You do. And I'd like to change that. My offer still stands."

"Why are you here, Lance?"

"To take your troubles away."

"Hardly."

"I heard about your water issue. Tough break. I see you've got it all cleaned up, but you haven't opened your doors."

"We'll be back open tomorrow."

"Good. Having a clearance sale I presume."

"Excuse me?"

"Your store shelves are nearly empty. I simply assumed you were liquidating your inventory."

"Not at all. We're stocked up and ready to go."

"I see. Is that really your best play?"

"I don't follow."

"Mr. Klein, I'll be frank with you. I met with your banker. We go way back. I heard about your loan. Well, your attempt at a new loan. I know you're on the ropes. I'd like to help you."

"Taking my store isn't helping me," Edwin said.

"But it's not really your store, now is it?" Massey said, spitting out the words. "I know your story. You're not a toy man. There is no such thing anymore. The big chains have swallowed up these rinky-dink stores. You have no buying power. You can't make it. You don't want to be here, but yet you refuse my offer of help. I question your motivations Mr. Klein."

"Well, I don't question yours," Edwin said. "I know you bought the other buildings on this block. You can use all the fake corporate names you want. I know I'm your lone holdout. Let me save you some time. I will not sell the building. Period."

"You can make all the defiant declarations you want, but the fact remains, I can simply wait you out. Is that what you want?" Massey asked with a smirk. "You won't last until the New Year. I've heard about your financials. Would you rather lose the store and end up with nothing? Or would you like to get out while you still can? You'll be able to pay off what you owe here and still walk away with enough to start over someplace else. Just not on my block."

Edwin didn't respond. Massey continued.

"I'll give you four more days—until Christmas Eve—to make a decision," he said. "After that, I'm coming after you, and you will lose everything. It's your choice."

The bell on the front door rang as Edwin thrust it open.

"Get out of my store," he demanded.

"I'll see you in four days, Mr. Klein," Massey said, "I didn't want it to come to this."

"Get out," he repeated.

Edwin shut and locked the door, then walked to the back room and sat at his ratty desk. What the hell am I doing, he wondered?

The brown bottle of whiskey called out his name. He unscrewed the cap, grabbed the coffee mug and waited. He didn't pour the booze into the cup, but he wanted to so badly. He wanted to be lost again. Who could blame him? If anyone deserved a little break from reality, surely it was he. He thought back to what Amelia asked him in the church. Was this really who he had become? A drunk who couldn't deal with reality? He wondered why her comments had stayed with him and why they felt so powerful at this moment. A wave of guilt hit him.

He put the lid back on the bottle and set it back down. He still held the mug in his hand. He stared at the bottle for a long while, reading the label over and over until his eyes couldn't focus any longer.

Screw it.

He picked up the bottle, unscrewed the cap and placed his lips on the opening.

When the liquid hit his lips, it tasted like bile. He spit it out in disgust from both the taste and with himself for giving in yet again.

With all the strength he could muster, he threw the bottle against the wall. It shattered into a million pieces and dripped poison all over the back room, where earlier that day boxes of Christmas decorations had sat.

He ignored the mess and walked to the front of the store, determined to move on. Move forward.

* * *

He worked on the display window until the sun came up. In just a few hours, the store would reopen. When he was finally finished, he unlocked the front door and walked outside. It had stopped snowing, but the street and sidewalk were still covered in a fresh blanket of white stuff. The morning light pierced the window as Edwin stood facing his store from across the street. His body shook from the cold. He had neglected to wear a coat.

The window looked perfect. He'd followed Mary's instructions to the letter, placing each item exactly where she'd requested. When something didn't make sense, he used his instinct and just made it up. The scene was pretty familiar, after all.

To most people, Mary's scene was a simple one; Santa delivering presents to a home on Christmas Eve. But Edwin knew that Mary's designs, just like her mother Harriet's designs, were never that simple. This living room was unique. It told a story, even if only the designer knew the tale. But he knew too. The scene was a replica of Mary and his living room from their first Christmas together.

Edwin had brought home a small fake Christmas tree that first year, knowing that they didn't have the money to get a real one. They had decorated it together and Mary seemed satisfied at the time, but he knew she wanted a real one. She wanted the smell of the pine and the mess that it would leave on the rug. She'd always had a real one growing up, but it wasn't in the budget for the newlyweds.

He'd caught her looking at the little fake tree, but not with happiness. She wanted something more and it really wasn't too much to ask. So days later he borrowed some cash from Mary's dad Mr. Z and bought a real tree from a lot near their apartment. It was an outrageous sum indeed, but worth every penny.

When Mary came home that night, her face lit up like the sun. She raced over to Edwin and jumped in his arms.

"It's beautiful," she told him. "Thank you."

"I thought we should decorate it together," Edwin said.

"We don't have any more decorations," she said, smiling. "They're all on the little tree."

"Then let's take them off."

"No. You can't un-decorate a tree before Christmas," she said. "There's like a law or something against that."

"Then we need to buy some more decorations."

"Maybe not," she said.

Mary left Edwin standing alone by the tree. When she returned she was holding a large white star with blue sparkle lights.

"The fake tree couldn't hold this tree topper, so I just put it away."

Edwin used a step stool and placed the star on the new tree, hiding the extension cord down the back by the wall. Mary plugged it in and they both stood there, holding hands, looking at the light from the star illuminating their naked tree. The branches were still moist from the cold and snow outside, making them shine under the star.

"I think it's perfect just like that," Mary said.

"Me too."

Nineteen

Amelia stood behind the register going over the instructions Edwin had given her on how to operate the machine. Two hours after the store opened, she had yet to put her skills to the test. A few customers wandered in and asked for specific items.

"Do you have the Extreme Auto Bandit video game?" A frantic woman asked.

"No," replied Edwin, in an apologetic tone. "We don't carry video games."

"Well, that's a shame," she said in a terse tone.

He offered her several other educational options, but the woman was dead-set on getting her son the game he'd been begging her for since his birthday last November.

Another customer asked for a doll that pushes a baby stroller.

"I'm sorry," Edwin said. "That's an exclusive line that is only carried at Big-Mart stores."

This time Edwin didn't even have a chance to offer an alternative. The woman spun on her heal and exited the store in a huff. The two women were the only customers all morning, but of course, they didn't buy anything.

There were times when Amelia was working at the diner back in Bonners Ferry that hours would pass without a customer. Then some trucker hauling lumber through town would stop for a cup of coffee and maybe a meal. When the place was slow that meant tips were slow and she had a hard time making ends meet. No customers, no money. She felt the same way watching Edwin.

Edwin looked lonely, sorry and worried. She wished there was something she could do for him, but he hadn't even made eye contact with her in over an hour. He just stared out the window. She was uncomfortable.

Edwin stood a few feet back from the front door, his hands clasped behind his back surveying each passerby. Even for Edwin, this silent treatment was odd. Another hour passed and no one else came in.

At noon on the dot Edwin turned the open sign to closed, locked the door and pulled the window shades. Amelia stepped out from behind the register and Edwin met her in front of the counter. He was standing so close. She could see the pain in his wonderful blue eyes. She could smell the coffee on this breath. Not booze, but coffee. It made her happy.

The closed shades meant the store was only illuminated by the faint overhead light and the over-the-top holiday decorations. It created a warm glow.

Amelia's pulse began to race. Edwin reached out and touched her arm, lightly brushing her elbow. Just as quickly he pulled his hand away, but he didn't step back. Their faces were mere inches apart. Amelia prepared herself for what she thought would be their first kiss.

"It's OK," she said. She mimicked his touch, putting her hand on his arm, but this time slipping down to his hand. She grasped it and he returned the squeeze.

She closed her eyes and craned upward, preparing for his lips on hers, but they didn't come.

She opened her eyes. Edwin was looking at the backroom, a puzzled look on his face. He wasn't even looking at her. She blushed, embarrassed.

"We need to change the game," he said. "How much do you know about computers?"

"Um, some, I guess," she said. That certainly wasn't what she expected him to ask her.

"That's more than me," he said. "We've got a lot of work to do."

"On what?"

"The big sale."

"Sale?"

"Our holiday blow out," he said.

"I'm going to need a few more details than that."

"I've got it all worked out, I just need to write it down," he said, taking a step back, realizing for the first time that they were holding hands.

He looked down at their hands and then up to her. He smiled and didn't pull away.

"Let's get to work," he said.

Edwin dashed into the back room, leaving Amelia to wonder what had just happened between the two of them. He hadn't even noticed her.

Twenty

Lance Massey sat at the weathered brown counter of the Bottom's Up Tavern. The place was blue-collar hell and located near an industrial park. Men in coveralls and steel-toed boots were sprawled about the place, guzzling cheap mass-produced American beer and shoving fistfuls of stale popcorn into their mouths, leaving the telltale sprinkles of crumbs and salt on their unshaven faces. It disgusted Massey's refined tastes.

To his utter surprise the dive bar had Stella Artois on their sticky, smudged plastic menu. He ordered a glass, pleased to find anything to his liking. When the bartender returned he plopped down a green bottle, and cracked open the top with a bottle opener shaped like a hula girl. The cap spun off the bar top and onto the floor, never to be seen again.

Never to be seen again—exactly his thoughts when he walked into the bar. Why his private investigator had selected this place to meet was a mystery unto itself. Royce Tidau knew Massey would squirm in a place like this, which was probably the only reason he selected it. The enormous man took perverse pleasure in putting Massey in his place. While Massey didn't have the man on retainer, Royce did enough work for him that he didn't have to accept many new clients. He did the occasional job for his list of connections, but for the most part, Massey had Royce to himself.

He'd found the man to be extremely resourceful over the years, proving his worth time and time again when Massey needed an obstacle eliminated or at least circumvented. His ways were simple—research, persuasion and action. The research was solid and legitimate—the tradecraft of any PI. The persuasion and action, on the other hand, were what Massey paid the big bucks for. Sometimes it was a simple threatening phone call or anonymous letter in the mail with photos of some dope's brat kids. But Royce got his hands dirty too. And that's where the broken fingers, cut brake lines and arsons came into play.

Royce was a terrifying collection of capabilities, just waiting for the word to be unleashed for the right price. And Massey was all too happy to set him free.

Massey pulled a handkerchief out of his suit jacket pocket and wiped off the rim of the beer bottle, then the bottle itself. He stopped himself before starting to ask the bartender for a proper chalice into which to pour the Stella, knowing that the man would have no idea what a chalice was and why it was important to serving the beer. The round glass was designed to release the beer's flavor and aroma. The bottle, on the other hand, was an insult to the style of beer. He spun the bottle around on the countertop, watching the trail of icy sweat seep from the outside of the bottle to the counter. Then he noticed the bottle's expiration date was two months ago.

He held the bottle up to his nose and took a long sniff, trying to determine if the concoction had gone south yet.

"It's much more effective if you ingest the beer, not snort it," Royce said, hoisting his sizable frame onto the stool next to Massey.

Royce slapped him on the back, his standard hello for the man.

"I love this place," Royce said. "Feels like home."

In many ways Royce looked to be quite in his element, right down to the cheap beer he ordered, which he washed down with a shot of the house tequila. Massey was amazed with the man's demeanor and again questioned himself for putting up with all Royce's garbage.

"Can we just get this over with?" Massey said.

"Sure, sure, but you paid for the deluxe package, so I didn't want to rush you through it."

"I think I can manage."

Royce placed a faded black leather messenger bag on the countertop and removed a thin stack of papers and photos. He handed the stack to Massey who scanned the pages, but didn't take the time to read each one. To do so would prolong his visit to the Bottom's Up Tavern, something he did not wish to do in the slightest.

When he thought Massey was through reviewing his work, he ordered another beer and began to speak.

"I looked into your boy Edwin Klein," Royce said. "Seems like a stand-up guy except for the boozing, but hey, I'm not in a position to judge."

He held up his half-full bottle of beer to emphasize the point.

"You sure you want to take on the owner of a kiddie toy store? I mean we've done some pretty nasty stuff over the years, but kid's toys? Doesn't seem like our bag, my friend."

"I have never asked for your opinion in the past and I'm not about to start today . . . friend," Massey spat out the last word, knowing that the men were anything but friends. "I gave this clown a chance to bow out gracefully and he kicked me out of his store."

"Well, alright then, I can get back to work on him, if that's what you'd like."

"Oh, work on him, like you did with the flood? That wasn't what I had in mind when I told you to make sure he was out of business. A couple of puddles? He must have been terrified."

"Again, it's a kiddie toy store. You expected me to set the place on fire with a incendiary bomb?"

"You've done it before," Massey said in a hushed tone. Even in a dive like this, you couldn't really know who was listening in.

"Kids go in there, man. You can't torch it. And it's Christmas, too."

"When I pay you, it's Christmas," Massey said. "Until then you're my little elf who makes my gifts and my gifts alone. Got it?"

"OK, you're writing the check," Royce said "Well, not really a check, that would be stupid. Paper trail and all. You're in charge. So what's the game plan?"

"Nothing has changed from before. I need him out of business and off my block. I don't care how you do it, but I need that building empty by January. I can only hold on to the other properties through the first quarter of next year. Beyond that I'm too exposed financially and the whole deal falls apart."

"He's hanging on by a thread," Royce said. "You can see that in the documents there. Just wait him out a few more weeks and you can grab this building for a steal."

"No, I can't. If the building goes into foreclosure, then it's tied up for months or longer. Even with my contacts, I can't rush that process. I need to get him out before the building reverts to the bank."

Royce thought about that for a few minutes. Despite his gruff exterior, Royce was a softy when it came to kids. He didn't have any of his own, but he had twin nephews in Texas that meant the world to him. He'd done his reconnaissance work at Mr. Z's weeks earlier to stage the broken pipe and flood. He quite liked the place and didn't really like the idea of destroying it outright.

Mr. Z's toy store was just the kind of place his nephews would love. None of those overblown shoot 'em up toys—just educational stuff that a family could play with together. It was the kind of stuff Royce himself should have gotten when he was a kid, but never did.

But he wouldn't walk away from Massey either—especially not over this. The guy paid well and there was too much money to be made. Massey seemed to have an endless supply of projects that met his particular set of skills. He needed to be gainfully employed, even by a dirt bag like Massey. Besides if he didn't do it, then Massey would just find someone else.

"OK, I'll get your boy out. But I do it my way."

"Just get it done," Massey said, dropping a $20 bill on the counter and heading for the exit.

Twenty-One

Amelia and Edwin worked late into the night at her apartment. They had to speak in hushed voices so they didn't wake up Marcus and Susanna. The children had gone to bed early without one word of protest. Amelia had tucked them in while Edwin stayed in the kitchen working. Susanna requested a song and Amelia readily obliged, belting out a tune that was clearly some sort of inside joke between mother and daughter.

"You're really great with them," Edwin said.

"They're the only kids I have," she said. "I better be."

"I know, but they respect you and listen," he said, thinking of the playful give and take she'd had with Marcus that night. It allowed him to experience a true conversation with an adult, something many kids miss and end up resenting authority figures altogether.

But watching her talk with the children made him think of Mary and how she wanted kids so badly. Mary would have been a good mother too. She just never had the opportunity after having a miscarriage and then never being able to get pregnant again.

There wasn't a day that went by when he didn't think of Mary and he was thinking more and more about the letter she had left him. Yet the last few weeks, since Amelia had come into his life he knew that his thoughts stayed in the present more than in the past.

He wasn't sure what to make of this. Maybe it was just the natural progression of mourning because he was certainly still in mourning. It didn't mean he loved Mary any less. He just needed to move to a better place, a happy place like Mary suggested in her letter. He didn't know if Amelia was the person to help him with that, but he thought that she might be. He hoped she was, but it frightened him all the same.

Yet he couldn't help but wonder why Josh had left her and the kids. *Who does that?* He and Amelia had talked briefly about Josh while they completed the repair work in the store, but it didn't give Edwin a sense of the man. It was a story he was anxious to hear, but wasn't about to press her for details.

* * *

Amelia had severely understated her computer skills. Edwin watched in awe as her fingers danced across the keyboard, interrupted only by the movement of the computer's mouse. Mr. Z's had never had a full-blown company website—Mr. and Mrs. Z never found it to be a priority. Edwin and Mary had always wanted to enhance the simple placeholder webpage, but didn't have the knowledge or cash to pay someone to do it for them.

"Now, just remember, this isn't a transactional website," Amelia said. "I can't make one of those in just a few hours. This site gives a visitor an overview of the store, what you sell and where to find the physical location. If you want to add the ability to sell merchandise on the site, we'll need to hire it out."

"No this is fine for now," Edwin said. "We just need an updated page to put on the advertising."

She clicked through the pages for Edwin, who was watching over her shoulder. Amelia had taken photos of the store inside and out and created slideshows that showcased the store's best features, from the ornate woodworking on the railings, to the window displays, decorations and of course, the shelves of toys and games. To Edwin's delight the mom-and-pop features of the store showed really well on the site. He worried sometimes that the character of the store might turn some people off. People were used to the bright fluorescent lights of a big box store, not the unique charm Mr. Z's and other independently owned stores offered.

"Speaking of advertising," she said. "I sent the web banners to the local TV and newspaper websites. I also did a targeted search for desirable demographics on a few social networking and search engine sites, so that our ads show up when last minute shoppers search online."

"How do you know how to do all this?" Edwin asked.

"I took some classes online a few years back. There weren't a lot of opportunities to put it to use in Bonners Ferry. The computer had just been collecting dust. The web programming is pretty simple really, you just need to know how it all connects."

"I thought you were a waitress," he said.

"You can't wait tables your whole life."

"I'm glad you could do all this," Edwin said. "I couldn't do it without you."

"I know you couldn't," Amelia said, reaching up to his waist and playfully tickling him.

They shared a laugh, as Edwin's unfortunate weakness was revealed. He was terribly ticklish. Something he didn't reveal easily.

"It's my one character flaw," he said.

"Wow, that's impressive," she said. "You must be the perfect man."

"I've got a bum ticker too, but that's not as funny."
She gave him a stern look.
"No, it's not."
Amelia stood up from the kitchen table with a determined look on her face. She wasn't going to let this affectionate moment between them pass. They'd already missed a chance back at the store and that couldn't happen again. She clasped his hands inside hers and pulled him close. She craned her neck and their eyes met.

Edwin began to say something, but Amelia put her finger over his mouth to shut him up. They stood like that for a long moment. His aftershave was strong—she noticed he must have shaved before coming over. She took that as a good sign.

"Don't talk," she said.
"But—"
"We've talked enough," she said.

She moved her hand to the back of his neck and pulled his face down to her own. Their parted lips met in a soft kiss. Amelia pulled back slightly and saw that Edwin's eyes were wide and unfocused. She stepped back as Edwin clutched his chest. He collapsed to his knees on the kitchen linoleum, then down to the floor completely.

"Oh my God, Edwin," she said. "I'm so sorry."
Edwin shook his head and smiled.
"I'm OK," he said. "Really. My heart just gets racing when I get excited. If I don't take a break, I pass out. I'm OK."

He pulled her down onto his lap and wrapped his arms around her. His body was warm and inviting.

"So I got you too excited?" she said, playfully.

"You just surprised me that's all," he said.

"I'll be sure to make a reservation next time," she said, still looking worried.

"No reservation needed."

From their seated position next to the stove and kitchen garbage can, they shared several passionate kisses.

As Amelia ran her fingers through Edwin's hair, a curious thought popped into his head. He'd been out of the dating scene for so long that he didn't know what the next move should be—or if there even should be a next move. Was he supposed to stay at her apartment? Would he sleep over? What about the kids? Was there a lock on the door? Edwin didn't know what to do.

He felt like a teenager. He wasn't sure if he was ready for this—whatever it was.

Amelia seemed to notice his consternation.

"We've got a big day tomorrow finalizing this sale so we're ready to open the doors on Monday," she said. "You'd better get going."

She said it in a way that seemed to imply that she was interested in picking up where they left off, just not tonight.

Edwin let out an audible sigh of relief that made her laugh. He packed his things and kissed her goodnight by the door. What Amelia didn't see was Edwin clutching the railing outside her apartment and trying to once again catch his breath.

Twenty-Two

Edwin made it to the store about 8:30 on Sunday morning. The street was empty except for a city utility worker closing up a manhole cover down the street. The store had never been open on Sundays for one simple reason. Foot traffic downtown was low on Sundays and the store didn't get many customers. With the bad weather and constant dusting of snow, that still held true. People weren't out and about when they didn't have to be.

Each time he returned to the store he flashed back to the flood. He couldn't shake the feeling that the place may have somehow turned into an icy pond overnight even though the broken pipes were now safely repaired. When he flipped the lock and stepped into the dry, warm store, he felt relief. It might not be much, but at the moment, it was all he had.

He had tossed and turned all night, thinking about his time at Amelia's apartment. He was looking forward to spending more time with her, even just during store hours. During his restless night of sleep he was also trying to poke holes in his last ditch-effort sale. The sale was a stretch, but just might work. The flyers and advertising were done—they had done all that, but he needed to review the inventory and set aside some merchandise.

The two-day sale was simple. For every purchase made over $25, Mr. Z's would donate a new toy to the charity drive at St. Mark's Church. Pastor Isakson practically jumped through the phone when Edwin called to ask permission to name the church in the advertising.

"This is just the thing we need," he said. "Donations are down tremendously and many of these kids won't be getting anything for Christmas if not for our drive. This is wonderful, but can you afford it?"

"We're hurting too, I can't lie about it," Edwin said. "But I worked the numbers, if we can sell enough new product, the donations won't negatively impact us. Our main issue is getting people in the door. Once they get in the door, they tend to buy something, especially this late in the season."

The pastor and Edwin worked out all the logistical details. The sale would start Monday and end on Christmas Eve. The gifts couldn't be delivered until Christmas Eve since the sale would run until 3 p.m. on that day. Edwin needed that time to catch all the shoppers who procrastinated until the last minute and would be less picky about what they could buy—a good thing for a store with limited options. Edwin and Amelia would deliver the gifts to the church at 4 p.m., which would leave the church volunteers about an hour to wrap and prepare the gifts before the Christmas Eve service and the children's play.

The sale was a gamble, no question, but Edwin was all out of options. If this didn't get people into the store, then nothing would and he might as well hand over the keys to that lowlife Lance Massey. Not an option. If he was going to lose the store, he was going to go down fighting until the last possible second. The clock was ticking.

* * *

When Edwin left the store Sunday night he was nervous. It was to be expected. Everything was ready. Signs, prices and decorations. Edwin even picked out some peppy Christmas music to blast over the store speakers to get customers in the buying mood. He hung flyers in the lobby of every downtown building he could gain access to. People would see the flyers and come down, he was sure of it. Everyone waited until the last minute to shop, especially busy people who worked downtown. And to get a donation on top of a last-minute gift? It was perfect.

He locked the store and walked the block and a half to his car. His mind was focused on the sale and keeping the business alive. He could do it. He just knew he could. With his head elsewhere, he didn't notice Royce Tidau dressed in a city street worker's uniform pacing the back alley. And he certainly couldn't have guessed why he was there.

Twenty-Three

"You guys ready to go?" Edwin asked, holding up four tickets.

With the preparations for the store ready, Edwin had nothing left to do but wait until Monday morning for the store to open, which meant fretting all night long, something he wasn't looking forward to. So, he invited Amelia, Marcus and Susanna to a Spokane Chiefs hockey game to keep his mind off the pending sale. Marcus seemed a bit bothered that Edwin had elected to invite his little sister and mom to the game too, but his excitement to actually see a game in person made up for it.

From Edwin's side of things, he couldn't imagine what Marcus and he would have talked about during a two to three hour hockey game if Amelia wasn't around. He was good with families, with kids in the store, but one-on-one with a pre-teen was challenging. He just didn't have much experience in that area. Besides, he wanted to spend more time with Amelia and see where things went and this was a good way to do it.

The four of them piled into Edwin's beat up Nissan Sentra and drove downtown listening to the Christmas station on the radio. Well, most of them listened. Marcus immediately put on his headphones when he got into the car and zoned out from the rest of the group.

"I really appreciate you doing this," Amelia said.

"Sure, I told Marcus that I would get him to a game," Edwin said.

"No, not just the game. I mean this—us together. We haven't been out together and—"

Amelia cut herself off and blushed. Even in the darkened car, Edwin could tell that there was something else she wanted to say, but decided not to. He knew that most men wouldn't be interested in spending time with Amelia's kids. They'd prefer to have her all to themselves. This family-type outing was likely a first for all of them.

Edwin tried to fill the silence.

"When I was a kid, my uncle would take me to these games," Edwin said. "Not every game, but a few each year. He had this orange Volkswagen Beetle that he bought when he was overseas in the Air Force. I remember when he'd pick me up. The heater was this piece of junk. By the time we got down to the arena, I was freezing and the car was just starting to crank out a little bit of heat. He never even mentioned it, or noticed that I was shivering like a wet cat."

"We're you close to your uncle?" Amelia asked.

"As much as you might expect, I guess," he said. "He had kids of his own who were grown and busy. And he had my aunt, too. They were always off doing something and we really only saw them on holidays, mostly. But he certainly made an effort to include me."

"When you say 'we' you mean your parents? Are they in Spokane?"

Edwin hesitated before answering. He didn't really want to get into a discussion about his parents, especially in the short car ride to the game. He'd yet to say one word about them to Amelia as of yet.

"My mom is in South Carolina with her husband. My stepdad," Edwin said. "I'm not sure where my dad is. I haven't seen him since I was a kid."

Edwin didn't like talking about his dad because he didn't have much to say on the subject. When you don't know someone, you can't really describe them much. People tend to assume that all your relationships in life are based on the relationships you formed with your parents. He didn't buy into that. He'd been with Mary for many years and felt that if anything, she had a bigger influence on who he was as a person than his parents—especially his dad who he barely knew decades ago.

Norman Klein was a ranch hand. No more. No less. He met Edwin's mom Lucy at a 4-H livestock show. Lucy was in her teens and helping some of the younger kids show their animals to potential buyers. Norman was working for a rancher who wanted to buy several animals. She was from a well-to-do family and didn't have to work, while Norman was renting a room and barely making enough money to feed himself. But Lucy was infatuated with the wayward life of a ranch hand and they soon found themselves together and shortly thereafter—with child.

Lucy's family helped the young Klein couple purchase a little home near several farms, so Norman could be near the jobs he found suitable. But he didn't like being under their thumb, knowing that his livelihood depended on their generosity. He needed to be free to pursue his own life and didn't want the burden of a wife and young child dragging him down. He stuck around until Edwin was seven years old. The picture of the man in Edwin's head wasn't from memory. It was from an actual photograph, that's all he could remember.

The last time Edwin saw his father was the day after he graduated high school. His father had missed the ceremony and party altogether. No one expected him to come. He hadn't been invited, or heard from in years. So when Edwin saw a man wander into his employer's horse stables where he was mucking the stalls, he didn't expect it to be his father, in fact he didn't know who it was until he told his mom about it later that night.

The man, whom he didn't know was his father, had asked about the horses and who owned the stables. It was one of those encounters that didn't stand out until he realized later whom he was talking to. In the two minutes his father stood there he'd only glanced up at the man a few times. He was busy mucking the stalls after all.

Edwin imagined that his father just needed to see the man he had become. He was 18 and officially a man. But it was the cowardly thing to do, to lurk in the shadows and peek into your child's life. He hated his father for it. Hated that he didn't just disappear from his mind altogether. The photograph and the fuzzy memory of a stranger asking him questions in a horse stable weren't necessary. He knew his father as absent—that was it. He should have stayed that way and not tempted the hope that he could come back into Edwin's life. Not that he really wanted it anyway.

Edwin was his own man—not based on the absent nature of his cowardly father.

Edwin glanced back at Marcus in the backseat with his headphones on. He wondered how Marcus felt about his dad being gone too. At least when Edwin was a kid his stepdad was around. He wasn't the greatest guy in the world, but he came home every night and was fair to his mom and him.

Marcus didn't even have that anymore. He was on his own with just his mom. Josh must be some piece of work to leave such great kids.

"So you don't see your father?" Amelia asked.

"Not since . . . not in quite a while."

Amelia didn't press the issue and they rode the rest of the way in silence. Edwin paid for parking and they got in line at the turnstiles to get in. Once inside, Marcus took his ticket and disappeared into the crowd.

Edwin gave Amelia a questioning look.

"It's OK," she said, "He'll meet us at the seats."

Edwin wasn't sure why it was OK for an 11-year old boy to be given license to roam without supervision, but he held his tongue. It wasn't his son and he didn't want to rile the momma bear inside Amelia like the night they first met.

"Cotton candy! Please?" Susanna tugged on her mom's coat as they passed a vendor in a tall red-and-white striped hat with a cart stuffed full of cotton candy and other sugary concoctions.

Edwin didn't wait for Amelia to answer. He pulled out his wallet and bought two bags, giving one to Amelia and one to Susanna.

"What can I say? I like cotton candy too," he said.

Amelia tried to frown.

"You don't have to be up with her all night after she devours that whole bag in about four minutes."

"I guess I didn't think about that," he said.

Susanna gave him a big hug just above his knees—as high as she could reach.

"Thank you!"

"You're very welcome," he said. "Be sure to save some of that for your brother, OK?"

Susanna stuck out her lip in a pout, but took his hand and didn't let go as they wound their way through the crowd to their seats. They were on the upper level of the arena, behind the Chiefs net. When they arrived, Marcus was already in his seat, waiting for them. Amelia snuck Edwin a glance, as if to say, "I told you it would be OK."

Marcus sat on Edwin's left while Amelia sat on his right, followed by Susanna. The adults were in the middle and the kids on the outside. Throughout the first period of the game Edwin gave Marcus the rundown on penalties and simple game strategy. He wasn't an expert, but he'd seen enough games to get the general lay of the land and Marcus didn't know any better to contradict him. Marcus asked questions and cheered in the right places. When one of the opposing players tripped one of the Chiefs, a fight broke out among a handful of players near the net. The crowd was in an instant uproar, urging the players to continue pounding each other. Edwin and Marcus were on their feet cheering as the fight continued.

Amelia sat quietly with Susanna, who was coloring pictures with a small dry-erase board Amelia had brought, knowing the little girl would be bored out of her mind at the game. Amelia never once looked up to watch the fight, in fact anytime there was a scuffle at all, she'd return to helping Susanna with some element of her drawings, completely ignoring the cheers and violence. She didn't say a word about it, but Edwin could tell she didn't care for all the fighting.

They snacked on hot dogs and sodas during the first intermission. Edwin was surprised when Amelia put her hand on his knee, but he didn't show it. Without missing a beat he placed his own hand over hers and they instinctively intertwined their fingers. It felt good.

A photographer with a big flash on the top of her camera wondered through their section taking souvenir pictures of the fans in the crowd. Edwin had seen it before. The team would do a slideshow of the pictures to music during the second intermission to keep people entertained. They also email the fans a copy of the picture to keep.

The photographer eyed their group and made a beeline for them.

"Can the kids scoot in close to mom and dad for a picture?" she asked.

Amelia opened her mouth to say something. Presumably it was something like, "He's not their dad," but she stopped herself when both kids didn't miss a beat and leaned in close and smiled for the camera. The photographer snapped several pictures and took Amelia's email address.

"You have a lovely family," she said.

* * *

Amelia and Edwin sat next to each other on the couch after the game. They once again found themselves together in her apartment with two sleeping kids tucked away in their rooms. Despite the sugar rush, Susanna hadn't put up a fight. It helped that Edwin had carried her all the way from the car, up the two flights of stairs and directly to her bed. Marcus wanted to stay up with the adults, but didn't argue when he was told to brush his teeth and go to bed.

Amelia had offered Edwin a glass of wine, but immediately realized that offering him alcohol wasn't a good idea.

"Sorry, force of habit," she said.

"Don't worry about it," he said. "How about some decaf coffee?"

"I think I can handle that."

They each sipped their coffee. Hers was filled with sugar and creamer. His was black. Amelia had only put on a small pot, just enough so they could each have one cup.

"You nervous about tomorrow?" she asked.

"Not at all," he said, with little conviction.

"I am."

"What makes you nervous about a toy sale?"

"It's the first time my newly-discovered marketing and website skills are being put to the test," she said. "I hope I did everything right."

"Makes sense."

"Let's just assume you are nervous—just for the sake of argument," she said. "The best thing to do in situations like this is to keep a positive attitude. Good things don't just happen by accident. It's because somewhere, someone wished or hoped for that good thing to happen. Your positive energy helps that wish find its place."

"Sounds very Zen."

"Exactly. Whatever you put into the world will be returned to you," she said.

Edwin then wondered what exactly had he put into the world up to this point? What forces had conspired to cause Mary's death or to give him a heart defect? What did he put out there to cause the store to slowly slip into the red? Why were his returns so terrible?

"I'm not sure I believe in all that," he said.

"You don't have to," she said. "That's the beauty of it. Whether you're in control or not, it doesn't matter. Everything happens for a reason. We just don't always know what that reason is."

"Certainly not."

Edwin finished the last sips of his coffee and glanced at the clock. It was nearly midnight. The store would be open in ten hours.

"Maybe you should have made regular coffee," he yawned and stood up from the couch.

As he stretched his arms out, she could see his tight pack of stomach muscles. She sat there for a moment, imagining what they must feel like.

She hadn't felt this way about a man since the first few months she dated Josh. But she was just a kid back then and it could have been chalked up to puppy love. She was older now . . . and wiser. It wasn't supposed to be this easy to fall for someone, especially someone who was still mourning the loss of his wife and trying to dig out from underneath a failing business.

She couldn't shake how she felt. She should have isolated her children from even knowing he existed. That was the safe bet, but she wasn't playing safe with him. If everything happens for a reason, then there must be a reason that Marcus decided to shoplift at Mr. Z's and not the Big-Mart down the street. Maybe that reason was to bring Amelia and Edwin together.

She worried that if she came on too strong she'd scare him off, but she didn't want to hide it any longer.

"Stay here tonight," she said, putting her arms around his neck and pressing her body against his.

Edwin's mind flashed to the inevitable awkward moment the next morning when the kids saw him stumbling out of the bedroom, putting on the same clothes he'd arrived in the night before. There was a large part of Edwin that wanted to be with Amelia right at that moment. But yet another part of him was terrified to wake up in the same place as her kids.

"I told my neighbor Jonas that I'd let his dogs out tonight," Edwin lied. "And besides, I think we're both going to need a good night's sleep for all our customers tomorrow."

"OK," Amelia said, looking a little hurt. "You owe me."

"Yes I do."

Edwin couldn't shake the feeling that he'd just missed out on something very good.

Twenty-Four

Missoula, Montana

Royce dug through the nearly knee-deep snow and cut the chain-link fence at the ground line with a pair of bolt cutters. The cover of darkness and the remote location of the storage yard outside of Missoula was perfect for his shopping spree. He needed several items to follow through with Lance Massey's directives and he couldn't leave a paper trail to get them. Royce wasn't one to pay for things anyhow. Thankfully the natural gas supply company that served Missoula had just what he needed.

From a distance, he'd watched the facility empty out as regular business hours ended. By 5:35 p.m. there was only one light on inside the small office building located at the far corner of the storage yard. When that light turned off, a woman in her late 50s left the building, hopped into a pickup truck and drove away.

Now he had the place to himself, as long as he could wedge his large frame under the jagged fence in one piece. Not an easy task, but after a few minutes he made it through. He knew the break-in would be discovered at some point, but it didn't really matter. Considering the items he was stealing, and the 200 miles of distance between Missoula and where he intended to use the materials, it was unlikely the connection would be made for at least a few days. Even then, the theft would have no connection to him at all as long as he got in and out of the storage yard in one piece.

Once through the fence, he squatted behind a pile of yellow plastic and steel natural gas pipes of varying sizes.

The pipes had to be leftover scrap material, Royce surmised, otherwise the utility wouldn't have left them in such a disorderly fashion or exposed to the heavy snow and cold. He selected several steel pipes that were roughly three-feet long and tucked them under his arm. He followed a set of icy tire tracks to conceal his footprints as he briskly walked to the vehicle fleet area.

The first truck he came across had exactly what he needed and the doors were not locked. The perimeter security was supposed to keep people out, so the company didn't bother locking the trucks. Royce retrieved a hardhat from the passenger seat and snagged a handheld radio for good measure. He closed the door of the truck, placed the hardhat on his head and strode confidently toward the large beige warehouse building at the center of the storage yard. With the hard-hat on his head, the collection of pipes under his arm and now the radio clipped to his belt, he looked like he belonged if anyone happened to drive by and see him. His cover wouldn't last long if any company employees discovered him, but the place was empty and he didn't plan to stick around for very long.

When he reached the warehouse, he punched a five-digit code into the automatic garage door opener and waited for the green light to appear, signaling a proper code, which would allow him easy access to the warehouse. Earlier in the day he'd set up on the roof of a nearby building with a high-powered telescope and watched as several employees entered their personal codes for the door. He had three codes to choose from, just in case one of them didn't work. It was also entirely possible that he'd misread the codes, since most of the employees were wearing gloves and had mashed their fingers against the keypad to open it. He'd have to break into the building if the codes didn't work.

A red light flashed on the pad after the first code didn't work. He had memorized the numbers, but that wouldn't matter if he got them wrong in the first place. A flutter of panic spread through Royce when the second code didn't work either. It had only been seconds since he arrived at the pad, but any real employee would have entered by now. Royce also assumed the system had a failsafe that would lock down after several failed attempts. He tried to remember the third code. His finger hovered above the keypad. Just as he started to punch in the number, he heard the crunching of snow behind him.

A security guard holding a large flashlight stood just five feet to Royce's left. He was wearing a winter parka with a white patch on the left side of the chest that said Sure Thing Security. A rent-a-cop.

"Hey, you didn't check in at the office," the guard said. "You can't be back here with out punching in. How'd you expect to get paid?"

"Oh, man," Royce said in his best aw shucks voice. "I just needed to replace this length of pipe. I nearly left without doing it."

Considering that the guard was from a security company, Royce figured it was unlikely that he would immediately recognize him as a fraud. Maybe he could just talk his way out of this.

"Why didn't you just leave it in the truck and get it in the morning?"

Royce hesitated too long before answering.

"I need to see your ID badge," the guard demanded.

"It's in the truck," Royce said. "Can you just punch in the code for me? I'll drop these off and we can grab the badge."

"You're supposed to have it on you at all times."

"Have you ever dropped your badge in the snow up here? Then try to find it again, tracing your steps?"

The guard considered this for a moment.

"OK, I'm ready to get inside anyway. It's too damn cold out here."

Royce stepped back from the keypad as the guard punched in his code and the large door opened to the warehouse. The two men stood side by side as the door slowly rose and locked into place. There was no way now that Royce would be able to retrieve the items he needed from the warehouse with the guard as his chaperone.

"I've gotta grab some fittings to," Royce said. "It might take a minute. How about I just meet you at the office with my badge when I'm done."

"Sorry, I can't leave you alone if I can't verify who you are," the guard said as the men reached the inside of the building.

"I wish you wouldn't have said that," Royce said, spinning toward the man.

Royce dropped all but one of the steel pipes, causing the guard to jump backwards further inside the building. Royce gripped the last pipe in his right hand and lunged at the guard, narrowly missing his head. The guard pulled up his long winter parka and clutched at something on his belt. He backpedaled as he fumbled with the oversize coat as Royce advanced on him. The guard tripped and fell backward.

Royce stood over the man and raised the metal bar over his head. Just as Royce was about to slam the bar down, the guard finally removed his pepper spray that he'd been trying to remove from under his parka.

The foamy spray burned Royce's eyes and stung the inside of this mouth and nose. But he'd been pepper-sprayed before and he knew the effects were only temporary. If he didn't act now, the guard would get away, or worse, manage to subdue him until the police arrived.

With his eyes closed Royce slammed the bar down toward where he thought the guard was scrambling away. The blow was met by the pinging sound of hitting concrete. Undeterred, Royce thrust the bar down again, but this time he hit something relatively soft and felt a sickening crunch. Royce still couldn't see, but he knew the guard stopped scrambling away. He reached down for the bar and found it sticking straight up. He ran his fingers down the bar, until they met the eye socket of the security guard. The bar had made a direct hit to the man's eye and then into his brain, killing him instantly.

Royce slumped on the floor. It didn't have to be this way, he thought. Where did this guard come from anyway? Royce tried to rub the spray out of his eyes, but it was no use. It burned like hell. Luckily for him, the guard hadn't had the chance to unload the entire can of spray on him. His right eye had it worse than his left.

Peering out from his one good eye, Royce hit the inside keypad to close the large door. No use exposing himself any more than he already had. With the door closed he stumbled around in the dark for a sink to wash out his eyes. It didn't help, but after a few minutes, he could at least see again.

He rolled the guard on his side and pulled out the man's wallet. He'd try to make it look like a mugging or robbery gone wrong. He then removed his wedding ring after checking for any other jewelry. Damn it, he thought. The wallet showed a picture of the guard and his family. Royce tried to ignore what he'd seen, but the image of the dead guard and his happy family was burned into his memory. There was nothing he could do about it now. He needed to move.

Using the guard's flashlight, Royce wound his way through the warehouse until he found a room marked, "Chemical Storage." He smashed the small window beside the door and let himself in. Once inside he found an array of cylindrical chemical canisters, but he only needed the one marked "Mercaptan." The canisters were lined up on the cement floor by contents. It took him only a split second to find the one he needed. He loaded the canister onto a dolly and wheeled it to the side door of the warehouse.

He again used the icy tire tracks to guide his way through the storage yard until he reached the hole he'd cut in the fence. He laid the canister down near the fence, then slithered back through, dragging it with him.

He dropped the canister into the trunk of his car and headed for the freeway, already putting physical and mental distance between him and what he'd just done.

Twenty-Five

The line at the front counter of Mr. Z's was six-people deep and it was just 10:20 a.m. As soon as Edwin had opened the store, customers poured in. Some people had even been waiting outside. It was unlike anything he'd ever seen. It was as if a time machine had transported the store and all its customers back to Mr. Z's heyday of popularity before the big box stores stole all the customers. The Christmas music was playing and the joyous laughter of customers filled the store. Edwin couldn't wipe the grin off his face. It was amazing. He'd saved the store. It was that easy.

"I'm glad to see you guys up and running again," a man said as Edwin rang him up at the register. "I nearly forgot about this place until I saw that flyer this morning in the lobby of my office. My wife usually does all the shopping, but I figured it was for a good cause. You know, for the kids and all, so I'd come in."

"I very much appreciate it, sir," Edwin said. "And I hope to see you again."

The line of customers kept getting longer and longer, which worried Edwin because Amelia hadn't shown up that morning at 9:30 like she was supposed to. Now he was the only one manning the store. And since he had to work the register that meant no one was helping customers up and down the aisles. He tried to focus on the register, but he wanted to be in the aisles.

"Hey, bub, what are you playing at?" the man said to Edwin, as he held out his receipt.

"I'm sorry?" Edwin wasn't sure what the man said.

"You didn't give me my discount. What is this, some kind of scam? Man, and to think I was glad I came in here."

"I'm not sure what you mean," Edwin said.

"The flyer said I'd get a 40 percent discount if I spent 25 bucks," he said. "I'm looking at this receipt and I don't see no discount here."

Edwin was caught off guard.

"I'm sorry, you're mistaken," Edwin said. "We're not offering a discount on sales, just a donation to the St. Mark's charity drive for purchases over $25."

"Then it's a scam," the man said. "What a joke, and at Christmastime too."

He turned and stormed out of the store as the line of customers bunched closer together, partly to watch Edwin and the man, but also because the aisles were becoming crowded and they were running out of room.

"He's right about the discount," said the next customer in line, a woman holding a baby. "I saw it in the paper too. But don't worry about it for me. I'll still make my purchase."

"Thank you, but we never offered a discount," Edwin said, wondering what the heck had happened.

Someone down the line passed up a newspaper open to the advertisement for the Mr. Z's Last Minute Holiday Sale. Edwin braced himself on the counter. Stated as clear as day at the bottom of the ad read: "All sales will be discounted 40%."

He couldn't believe it. He proofed all the ads. He never said to put that on the advertisements or the flyers. That must be why Amelia didn't show up today. She knew she'd made a mistake and couldn't face him. How could she mess this up so badly?

Now what was he supposed to do? He couldn't very well argue with every customer in the store that his own advertising was wrong. He'd be laughed out of town. And he'd deserve it too. What a disaster.

To think that Amelia wouldn't even show up to face what she'd done. He tried to call her in between customers, but there was no answer. Incredible. He gave the discount to everyone who asked, which meant he was losing money on every transaction.

The noise inside the store started to hurt his ears. The Christmas music that was once so joyful and cheery now seemed hollow and contrived. The smiles on shoppers' faces turned into snarls as Edwin tried to explain that the discount listed on the advertising was a mistake. A stupid mistake that would probably finish off the store once and for all. Several people just left their items at the counter and walked out.

"Bait-and-switch scam," someone said. "How ridiculous in this day and age."

Edwin's heart was racing and he worried that he'd faint behind the counter. He wiped a layer of cold sweat off his forehead and tried to reassure customers that he wasn't running a scam. He tried to control his breathing, but his heart was pounding. It was times like this when Mary would take over whatever he was doing so he could calm down. She was always looking out for him.

Several people said they believed him and still bought merchandise.

"You need to fire your advertising agency, son," one man said. "That's a pretty big goof."

The store started to thin out, largely from customers abandoning their items. Edwin glanced at the clock—11 a.m. He'd only been open an hour and the day couldn't get any worse.

And then it did.

Twenty-Six

A man in a dark blue canvas Spokane Fire Department jacket stormed through the entrance of Mr. Z's waving his arms over his head to attract attention.

"I'm sorry folks, everybody out, nice and orderly like," the man said. "We've got a report of a pretty bad natural gas leak on this block and we need to evacuate until the utility guys can find the source."

The fireman held the door and stepped aside as people rushed out. Edwin could do nothing to stop his few remaining customers from leaving the store. Who could blame them? What toy is worth getting blown to bits in a gas explosion?

"You too, buddy," the man motioned to Edwin.

"But this is my store," he said.

"And it'll be your funeral too, pal. Move it. Make sure this place is empty, then head out."

Edwin did a quick check through the store and the balcony to make sure nobody was left inside. Not finding anyone, he grabbed his jacket, locked the front door and followed the rest of the crowd down Riverside Avenue and behind a line of yellow caution tape the fire department had set up. A crowd was gathered behind the line, apparently not concerned that they were mere inches from where the fire department claimed it was safe. Three fire engines idled nearby, their red-and-white flashing lights reflecting off the neighboring buildings.

Edwin noticed the rotten-egg smell, which he recognized as natural gas. A few summers ago, his neighbor Jonas had backed his camper into the gas meter on the side of his house. The utility company had to come out to cap it, but the awful smell filtered around his house even as the gas dissipated in the air. The smell in the air now was much stronger than what he remembered though.

He tried to call Amelia again, but her phone went right to voicemail, like she was already on the line. He left her a not-so-nice message about the advertising fiasco, telling her that he expected her to come into the store anyway. They needed to talk. And he needed the help explaining the situation to customers. He then realized that all his potential customers were standing around next to him anyway and wouldn't be buying anything any time soon since the fire department evacuated his block.

After just a few minutes the natural gas company truck pulled up and the fire department let them drive down Riverside, which seemed to be where the rotten egg odor was coming from. Edwin watched as a man in a yellow hard-hat and reflective vest adjusted a handheld device equipped with a wand and started to walk up and down the block. He held the wand at sidewalk grates, doorways and cracks in the pavement. After a quick pass he flagged down a fireman in charge of the evacuation and had a quick conversation. The fireman jogged back to the line of people.

"We gotta move this line back," he said. "Just as a precaution."

Someone in the crowd yelled, "What's going on? You need to tell us."

The fireman stepped back.

"The utility guy said the gas readings are pretty strong, but he couldn't immediately tell where the leak was coming from, so just to be safe we're going to move everybody back a bit," the fireman said.

More trucks from the utility arrived on the block. The employees huddled together and pointed up and down the street as several of them put on full-body fire-resistant suits.

Edwin leaned against the wall of a building away from the crowd. He needed to use this time to think up some way out of the jam he was in. The damage was already done. It was pretty unlikely, he thought, that the customers who were in his store when it was evacuated would return once the store reopened. Most likely they were last minute shoppers who would just go to another store that wasn't in danger of exploding.

In some ways the evacuation was a blessing since now he didn't have to explain the misprint in the advertising, but it also meant he wouldn't be selling anything at all. Even with a small profit he would have been making something, but not now. He thought back to what Lance Massey said—four days. Four days and the store would be beyond saving. That clock was now down to just two days and the longer the evacuation lasted, the fewer hours he had. He watched the minutes tick away as now more utility workers were pacing up and down the street with handheld devices.

The man who looked to be in charge of the utility company's response was standing close to the fire chief. The media was now on scene, reporting what little they knew. The snow started to fall and the uppity reporters started to complain about their hair. One of them called over the fire chief and Edwin took the opportunity to learn what he could. He caught the attention of the utility manager, who walked over to the caution tape where Edwin was standing.

"My store is down there," Edwin said. "What's going on?"

The utility manager had on a tan coat and wore a pleasant expression on his face. The danger of a gas leak didn't seem to bother him.

"We're reading low levels of gas up and down the block, which is a bit unusual," he said. "Normally the readings are higher in one particular place, but decrease as you move away from the source. That's not happening here."

"Can't you just shut off the gas?"

"If we shut it off before finding the source, we'll have a heck of a time finding the problem and we won't know what to fix. So that's not really an option."

"How long before I can open my store?"

"I wish I could tell you, but I just don't know."

One of the utility workers called for the manager back down the street.

"I'm sorry I've got to go, but as soon as we know more we'll let everyone know."

The man jogged down the street then entered the building next to Mr. Z's with another worker.

Standing here waiting would do him no good. He walked down a few blocks to a drug store and bought a black permanent marker. He then retraced his route from the previous day when he'd hung up the flyers. Building after building he found the flyer and used the marker to cover over the 40% discount lettering. He couldn't believe that he missed it before. He'd read through them so carefully, but there it was, plain as day. Amelia typed it in, and he approved it. He was exhausted. He even thought the flyer was printed on yellow paper, but all the flyers he saw were white paper. He was losing it for sure.

He called the newspaper too, but they didn't have room to place a new ad to run on Christmas Eve. It wasn't enough notice and they were short staffed because of the holiday. He didn't know where to start with the web ads. That was Amelia's department. So they would have to run as is.

After he made his calls and fixed all the flyers he returned to the fire department's barricade. A utility worker was using a jackhammer to break open part of the street. Edwin brushed off the newly fallen snow on the curb and took a seat, prepared to wait all day if he had to.

* * *

From across the street, Royce watched the chaos that he had caused for Edwin Klein and dozens of fire and utility workers. In the pre-dawn hours of the morning Royce had used a commercial landscape sprayer and coated every few feet of the Riverside Avenue with mercaptan, the natural gas additive scent. For good measure, he sprayed several areas of Howard and Stevens streets as well.

Natural gas alone was odorless and colorless, so gas companies added the rotten egg-smelling chemical mercaptan so the gas could be detected by smell if it leaked. It was a safety thing. He spread a concentrated amount of the chemical on the ice and snow, but also soaked several sponges with a mixture of water and mercaptan and shoved the sponges into storm drains and rain gutters. In one building that wasn't locked he poured the chemical on a heating unit, which quickly spread the smell throughout the entire building.

The previous day he'd also donned the suit of a street worker and descended into the depths of the street, looking for possible locations to store or unleash the odorant. He found a set of water pipes that, despite the cold weather, were dripping with sweat. He expected frost outside the pipes, but water in the pipes was warmer than the outside temperature, thus the sweat. He'd coated the pipes and watched as the steam floated up into the vast abyss of pipes the fed into the many buildings up and down the street. It would take hours for the utility company to discover that there was no gas leak whatsoever, in fact, Royce couldn't even tell if the street was plumbed with a gas line at all. He wouldn't even know what to look for, but that wasn't really his concern. His key job was to keep Mr. Z's closed.

When Lance Massey had ordered him to make sure Mr. Z's shutdown, it would have been simple to set a fire and destroy the building or even to stage a robbery late in the day to steal any cash profit Mr. Z's had made. But he didn't want to hurt anyone unless he had to. Especially not in a kids toy store. That would be bad karma. The guard in Missoula was the exception. Royce's back was too the wall and he had no other choice but to end the man. The fact remained that Royce had driven two states away to get the material he needed so he didn't have to put anyone in danger. The guard didn't deserve to die, but Royce had no remorse for his actions. It was the cost of doing business and he'd do it again if he had to.

The workers down the street were now digging a second hole and looking perplexed. He granted himself a hard-earned smile and then turned his attention to Edwin Klein, who was looking more defeated than ever before.

Twenty-Seven

At 4:30 p.m. the fire department announced that the block was all clear of any natural gas leak. The utility company had found several of the sponges and had chalked the whole thing up to an elaborate prank, although the rationale for such an act was unclear. They were still stationed on the street checking their pipes as a precaution, but the evacuation was lifted and traffic on the street resumed as normal. Edwin had patiently waited behind the caution tape the entire day, ready to open his doors the moment he was allowed to do so. Now that he had the opportunity, he wasn't in much of a hurry.

A man doesn't rush to his own funeral, Edwin thought as he stood waiting to cross the street. He couldn't cross it. He just stood there staring at the window scene of his first apartment and its two ridiculous trees. He thought of Amelia, not Mary, which made him ashamed. He should be thinking of Mary, not his new friend. Especially when she abandoned him when he needed her the most.

He caught his own reflection in the window as he unlocked the door. The bags under his eyes were dark and his face was drawn. Over the past few months he'd spent so much time worrying about the business that he would often forget to eat anything throughout the day. He even had to add a new hole in his belt to keep his pants from slipping down. He seemed to be wasting away. Circling the drain along with his business and personal life.

The store was warm inside. Edwin flipped on the lights and saw the place light up with all the decorations that Amelia and the kids had helped put up. The deep red Poinsettias and striped candy canes glowed throughout the store. The white LED lights reflected off the copper tiles on the ceiling. It really looked fantastic in the store. It was just missing inventory, customers and cash. Pretty pictures don't pay the bills.

Edwin locked the front door and flipped off the lights. He went into the back room and was glad that he'd smashed his only bottle of booze against the wall days earlier. He wasn't strong enough to resist that simple temptation. He needed the quiet so he took the phone off the hook. In his exhaustion he'd failed to notice the blinking message light. As soon as he lifted the receiver the light disappeared. He cleared a collection of cardboard boxes off the faded green couch and didn't decide to take a nap, it just sort of happened. He sat down and was fast asleep as soon as his head hit the couch cushions.

* * *

Lance Massey arranged the meeting this time. No more close encounters with the riff-raff that Royce hung around with. It was time to make his contractor feel just as uncomfortable as he had been just days before in the God-awful bar. Royce worked for him after all.

When Royce arrived at the Davenport Hotel lobby in downtown Spokane, he found Massey in a high-back chair near the enormous fireplace at the west end. He was swirling his glass of Gin and Tonic with a little red plastic stick.

The marble floors and opulent surroundings made Massey feel at home, if not a bit jealous. The Davenport

Hotel was the crown jewel of elegant accommodations and events in the region. His hotel and retail development, just two blocks away would put it to shame, if he could only get control of Edwin Klein's store.

To Massey's surprise, Royce was dressed in slacks, a sport coat and a quite fashionable brown fedora. He was carrying a long overcoat to complete the ensemble. The goon didn't look out of place at all, which only served to upset Massey.

"Nice threads," Massey said. "You got a date or something?"

"You're not my type," Royce said without missing a beat. "No offense."

Massey took a drink to hide his displeasure from the smarting remark.

"I think I was pretty clear about Edwin Klein," Massey said. "He needs to be out of business, now. What are you waiting for?"

"You said I had until January," Royce said. "And besides, this guy's a good as gone. Did you see what happened today?"

"Why, because there was a gas leak on his block?" Massey said.

"You don't think that happened by accident do you?"

"That was you?"

"One of my best stunts, even if I can't take credit for it publically. I should get a medal for that one, especially for the planning. Man. That was a piece of brilliance."

Royce explained how he obtained the materials and how he had to "pop the guard" to get out clean. Massey considered this for a moment and tried not to admire

Royce's creativity. He couldn't care less about some security guard in Montana.

Royce's evacuation plan was just a temporary fix. What he needed were assurances that Edwin Klein was gone, not just smoke and mirrors.

"I made some not-so-helpful modifications to their advertising campaign too, but I'm not sure if that panned out or not. The store was evacuated before I could go in and take a listen."

"Are you afraid of this man?" Massey asked. "Because from where I'm sitting I see that you're just pussy-footing around. What am I paying you for, other than to end this?"

"I told you that I would do this thing my way. Have I failed you before?"

Massey knew Royce was as reliable as a man in his line of work could be.

"I'm not sure how much more simple I can make this for you," Massey said. "Edwin Klein is a pest who is holding up a deal that could be worth tens of millions of dollars. Dollars that neither you nor I will ever see if you don't get your ass into gear."

"Our payment arrangement has already been negotiated," Royce said. "You don't want to threaten me, Lance."

"It's not a threat, I'm simply clarifying our terms. You already 'popped' one guy. Klein's a sitting duck. What's one more for your collection?"

Twenty-Eight

Christmas Eve

Edwin opened the store at 8 a.m., far earlier than it had ever been open in the store's history, but today had to be a historic kind of day. He'd slept at the store and was ready to go. He fueled up with an entire pot of coffee and was buzzing when the first customers came in. The pace was steady, but still slow. A few purchases here, a few there. Only two people asked about the 40% discount, but didn't argue when Edwin said that promotion was no longer valid. He hated to say it that way, but he didn't want to get into a he-said-she-said type of discussion. Thankfully, everyone was in the Christmas spirit—or at least the spirit of giving. The pile of toys for Pastor Isakson and St. Mark's Church was growing as well, which made Edwin happy.

He kept busy throughout the morning by helping customers and preparing donation boxes. His tasks distracted him so much that he hadn't put a great deal of thought into why Amelia had once again failed to show up at the store and had yet to return any of his calls. Maybe it was all just too much for her. Entering a relationship with a man she barely knew, who was losing his business on top of fighting the bottle; there were practically flashing lights around him that said 'stay away.' He forced himself to focus on his work and not dwell on what might have been with Amelia. Her absence said volumes about their future anyway. It didn't make him feel any better.

There wasn't one seminal moment that told Edwin his store was finished. He didn't have a dollar figure in his head of what he needed to make that day to keep the place afloat. Had he made those calculations, he would have realized that no amount of sales could really turn things around.

As the realization that Mr. Z's would be closing for the last time hit him, he was overtaken by a sense of peace and calm. He'd done his best to keep the store alive. He'd done Mary proud, even in his failure.

Feeling as though a massive weight had been lifted from his shoulders, Edwin focused on stuffing every toy he could fit into the massive cardboard boxes he'd ordered to deliver the toy donations to the church. An occasional customer would arrive at the store on a mission to get a last-minute gift. Edwin treated each of them like royalty and thanked them for their business as they left. The end was near, but he didn't want anyone's last impression to be a negative one.

At 11:30 a.m. on the dot, there were eight people, including himself, inside the store. A grandfather who came in alone was looking at board games. A mom and her two daughters were browsing the doll aisle. And Edwin was helping a young couple find some basic reading books for a first grader on their Christmas list.

A man in a long overcoat, a brown fedora and dark black sunglasses entered the store. Edwin greeted him with a wave. The dark glasses were an odd choice, he thought, but quickly returned his attention to the young couple and their book needs.

The two blasts from the man's handgun went directly into the wooden floor. The shots rattled the store's windows and shook the ground with a violent jolt. The store's patrons erupted in panic. Nearly every one in the store instinctively dropped to the ground. Everyone except Edwin.

The mom in the doll aisle pushed her daughters behind her as they all crumpled to the ground. The grandfather simply folded to his knees. The young couple at Edwin's feet scrambled down the front aisle and hid behind a display rack.

Edwin didn't scramble away or cower in fear. He stood, straight as an arrow as the gunman pointed the steel gray gun at his head. The man's words were slow and deliberate as he advanced on Edwin, placing the barrel of the gun on his temple.

"Everyone be cool and this will be over very shortly," he said, in almost a whisper. "No heroes."

Edwin studied the man's face, which was just feet from his own and partially disguised by the large sunglasses.

The girls hiding underneath the cover of their mother's arms were crying loudly. The gunman moved his head ever so slightly and watched them, but the gun never left Edwin's head.

Mr. Z's had been robbed years ago and Edwin knew that Lloyd Zimmerman used to keep a 12-gauge shotgun under the front counter "just in case," he said. But one day a precocious young boy snuck behind the counter and emerged with the gun in hand, telling his mom, "I want this one!" It was the last day Lloyd kept the gun under the counter. Edwin was defenseless against this man.

The seconds crept by, but the gunman didn't say a word. It seemed as if he was waiting for something or debating what his next move should be.

Edwin could feel his heart racing and blushed, thinking that this exact moment would not be a good time to faint. He needed to get this man out of the store and away from him and his few remaining customers.

"Let me open the register for you," Edwin said. "You can have whatever you want, just please don't hurt anyone."

Edwin could feel the man's face harden, even behind the sunglasses.

"I didn't come here to rob you," he said.

* * *

The knot in Royce's stomach was twisting and turning like a rollercoaster on fire. His left shoulder was aching from extending the Beretta straight out into Edwin Klein's face. He tried to focus on the man he was sent to kill, but the screams and cries of the two young girls down the next aisle kept diverting his attention. He was scarring them for life. They would always live in fear that someday the man in the brown hat would kill one of them too. He'd done it before, right in front of their eyes on a Christmas Eve they would never forget. Couldn't forget.

But there was no turning back now. He'd made the agreement with Massey. Royce was a killer after all. That was his value. His identity. If he couldn't do this job then what would he do? Word would leak that he couldn't be trusted to take care of business. He'd be ruined—all because he couldn't terminate some toy store owner who nobody would miss anyway. And Royce had looked. Klein had no wife or kids and no other dependants to speak of, yet there was something about this man and this store that made Royce pause.

He couldn't do it. Not here.

If Klein had simply gone home last night as Royce had expected, then he would have popped him in his sleep. He'd already cased his house and was waiting for Edwin to come home last night, but he never did.

But Plan B wasn't working out. And then Klein himself gave Royce the acceptable out he needed. At least ruin another day's profit by robbing the place.

"Yes. Open the register and give me all the cash. No funny business."

Royce stepped backward toward the door and counter, putting a little distance between himself and Edwin. Edwin kept his hands raised with his palms facing outward until he reached the register. The machine clicked and dinged as the drawer opened.

Edwin collected the little cash he had and placed it in a bright green store-branded Mr. Z's plastic bag. He held out the bag.

"You expect me to walk away from a robbery, holding an advertisement of the store I just robbed? Just put the money on the counter and back up."

Edwin did as he was told. Royce scooped up the small stack of bills and shoved them into his coat pocket.

"Today's your lucky day, Mr. Klein," he said. "You get to see tomorrow. Merry Christmas."

Royce's head was reeling as he considered the ramifications of what he'd just let slip through his fingers. He couldn't help but let out a forced belly laugh as he exited the store, for theatrics more than anything else.

"Merry Christmas to everyone!"

The bell on the door clanged as he walked briskly out of the store and turned east. He shoved the sunglasses into a pocket of his overcoat, then removed the coat and fedora, balling them up under his arm. He then pulled a blue Seattle Seahawks stocking cap out of this back pocket and pulled it down low to his eyes. He dumped the coat and hat in a trashcan and lit a cigarette, walking at a comfortable pace. Now two blocks away, he flicked the cigarette and climbed the steps to the city's skywalk system that spanned much of downtown.

In minutes he was eating popcorn in the back row of a half-filled movie theater. An hour or so earlier, before the movie started, he'd taken his time and purposefully chatted with several movie theater employees in his blue Seahawks stocking cap. A few minutes into the movie he had walked out the back exit. If anyone wondered where he'd been, they would have likely assumed he was using the restroom. People aren't that observant anyway.

His popcorn was stale and his soda was flat, which disappointed Royce. He quickly got caught up in the movie and forgot about all the trouble he'd just caused at Mr. Z's.

Twenty-Nine

Edwin had to hand it to the Spokane Police Department. Unlike a month ago when they had failed to show up when Marcus had shoplifted at the store, this time they arrived just seconds after the robber left the store. The couple hiding in the back of the store had dialed 9-1-1 on a cell phone the first chance they got, but it was too late to catch the guy. He was long gone. The cruisers with their flashing lights reflected off the store windows. The officers took their reports and asked Edwin if he was all right after going through such a traumatic experience.

"I'm fine," was all Edwin could muster. He couldn't shake the feeling that he'd seen the man before, but for the life of him, he couldn't place him. The dark glasses obscured much of his face.

The reporters showed up soon after the police did. A young brunette reporter, fresh out of college, arrived with her cameraman and set up shop on the sidewalk in front of the holiday display window. She reported, "live from the scene of the crime" for several minutes. In between takes she complained loudly about having to work on Christmas Eve while fiddling with her phone. Her boyfriend was waiting for her at home. The veteran cameraman explained to her that Mr. Z's was a Spokane landmark and that people would care about the crime. It was important. She seemed indifferent and left at the first chance.

The newspaper sent someone over too, but he spent a little more time inside the store doing actual reporting. He talked with the police spokeswoman, who provided him all the tired message points about "finding the perpetrators of the this heinous crime that has rocked our community." He talked with some of the customers who were still hanging around the store. And finally he talked to Edwin, getting the full picture of what occurred inside the store just moments earlier.

"Do you plan on adding security cameras or any other security measures, now that your store has been robbed?" he asked.

"No, there's no need for that now," Edwin said.

His lack of emotion and energy wasn't lost on the newspaperman.

"Is there anything else you need? Everything OK? I can only imagine what you're going through."

"The only thing I need right now is for all these people to get out of my store so I can get my donations ready for St. Mark's," Edwin said.

He explained the sale and how he'd hoped that it would have brought in much-needed customers. They peered into the toy bin of donations for St. Mark's. There were only a few toys waiting.

"Business has been pretty slow?" the reporter asked.

"A crawl."

"It shouldn't take you more than a few minutes to pack up those toys though."

"Yes, but that's not all that's going," Edwin said.

"There are more donations somewhere else?"

"Yes. It's all going," Edwin said.

"Excuse me?" he asked.

"Today when I close the doors of Mr. Z's, it will be for the last time. I'm giving away everything in the store."

* * *

Edwin didn't know what Twitter was and he didn't have a Facebook page. He didn't understand how the news of something could spread like wildfire through social media, with interested people sharing, retweeting and forwarding on the news until everyone they knew online was aware of something. The Spokane Chronicle reporter sent out a message on Twitter telling his audience that the owner of Mr. Z's needed immediate help boxing up everything in his store. Everything. The news flooded the Spokane area.

Within 30 minutes, dozens of people who Edwin had never met, arrived wearing gloves, ready to help. They left their Christmas Eve dinners sitting at home to get cold. Entire families, together just for the holiday, loaded into their cars and drove downtown to lend a hand.

"Mr. Z's is really closing?" they asked him repeatedly.

"I'm afraid so," he said over and over.

"I used to come here as a kid," more than one person said.

The young brunette reporter returned to her spot on the sidewalk, this time reporting of the "miracle of the holiday season." The distain on her face was gone. The other two local TV stations soon joined her. They did live shots in and outside of the store, capturing every moment. The police returned too, directing traffic down Riverside Avenue as curious onlookers and volunteers spilled out onto the street.

Soon there was no place to put all the boxes of toys without blocking the front door. There were just too many people inside the store. It was like nothing Edwin had ever seen before. He shrunk into the background as several people took leadership roles, directing the packing of boxes, sealing them up and stacking. A group of the volunteers started a bucket brigade to get the boxes, carried by hand, down to St. Mark's two blocks away.

Two people were stationed on each block, carrying the boxes halfway, then handing them off. The police held up traffic at each intersection so the boxes didn't stack up on the snowy sidewalk.

Not expecting such a massive amount of donations, St. Mark's was completely unprepared to handle the sorting and wrapping of presents. Edwin, recognizing that this might be the case, sent some of his volunteers as reinforcements. The only thing that slowed them down on their way out the door was the line of people giving Edwin big, tear-filled hugs. The TV cameras saw it all, beamed live, not that Edwin or any of the volunteers cared to notice.

One of the cable news networks, searching for a feel-good holiday story to run on the traditionally slow news day of Christmas Eve, broadcast the store's transformation to the entire country. It made the national evening news too. Mr. Z's was a victim of the tough economy, they said, but also a symbol for the human spirit.

From one reporter's tweet to television coverage nationwide, the closure of Mr. Z's was seen by millions of people in less than an hour. Millions of people who had never heard of the iconic Spokane store. Millions of people who would never forget its name.

When the volunteers took the last box out the front door, Edwin was alone in the store again. The reporters and crowd had followed the news down the street to St.

Mark's. He sat down cross-legged on the wooden floor and leaned back against the front counter. The twinkle lights still glowed over the holiday decorations that looked terribly inadequate to fill the empty store. One of the green garlands had come loose from the ceiling and hung like a rope to nowhere. The shelves were bare. Mr. Z's was closed.

Edwin couldn't hold back his heavy tears.

It was done. He felt relief.

Thirty

The spotlights from the TV trucks shone brightly against the white snow falling outside St Mark's. Reporters were stationed outside the church to do live updates on the Mr. Z's story—the store that gave everything for Christmas.

Dozens of children were either peeking outside the second story windows or hovering near the entrance watching all the surprise commotion. Tonight was supposed to be their big night as the Christmas play was to begin at 5:30 that evening.

The volunteers had already run out of wrapping paper for all the gifts from Mr. Z's. Once again, the call went out to people through social media and the donations of wrapping paper flooded the church parking lot. Some of the reporters forgot their unbiased bystander status and joined in the fun too.

Pastor Isakson paced down the long main aisle of the church as the children rehearsed the play for the final time before the show. He'd already received a request to film the show live on cable television. They wouldn't show all of it, the producer promised, just enough so people at home could get the feel of the event. After all, she said, the donations that everyone was so focused on were for these kids. He agreed to let them set up a camera as long as it wouldn't distract the kids.

Pastor Isakson quickly realized, as the camera crew constructed a stand and mounted a massive camera with a bright red light on it, that the camera would be anything but hidden from the kids.

He originally expected a handful of people to come to the play. The parents, if there were any, always came. And some of the church regulars would come, but that amounted to just a dozen people. Last year around 50 people total came. But this year, with all these people working to wrap presents or just stop by and see the chaos, he expected a full house. And now the camera was looming in the background. He continued to pace. The show was to start in two hours.

The kids seemed to sense something was different about tonight too, but he couldn't find any words of encouragement for them. These kids were as independent as any adult. They had seen rough times and were, unfortunately, already hardened to the realities of life. That's what made their performance so important. It was something to be proud of. Family and friends would forgive their missteps on stage, but now, with this circus raging outside, he was worried that any falter would simply crush them.

He shouldn't have been worried.

"I'm going to be a TV star!" one shepherd exclaimed when he noticed the camera.

"No one is going to notice the shepherds," said the boy playing Joseph as he tossed baby Jesus up, higher and higher into the air.

"Stop throwing around our Lord and Savior," Pastor Isakson said to little Joseph. "He's been through enough already."

Pastor Isakson gathered all the kids together in a side room, away from the cameras and reporters. Someone brought over trays of cookies and sweet bread for the kids. One of the volunteers made hot chocolate from the commercial-sized coffee pots. After a few protests about the hot chocolate tasting like coffee, the kids settled down. With bellies full of hot chocolate and cookies, the kids quietly watched Tim Allen in "The Santa Clause" on a TV mounted to the wall of the side room.

Pastor Isakson grabbed a chair and watched the movie too, happy to let his nerves cool.

* * *

Edwin donned his heavy coat and set off for St. Marks. He was greeted by a church volunteer who grilled him about what type of task he would be best at. She didn't know who he was and didn't care. There were lots of things that needed done, she said. He could wrap presents, sort them, or sell tickets to the show tonight. Edwin, not wanting to go near the presents, agreed to sell tickets to the Christmas play. Apparently they'd never sold tickets before, but with the crowd they expected tonight, Pastor Isakson gave them orders to capitalize on the moment.

He got a large manila envelope and a roll of red tickets.

"If anyone says then can't afford $2 for a ticket, then tell them to shove off," the woman said with no hint of irony.

"How many tickets can I sell?"

"I guess that depends on how good a salesman you are," she said.

The woman, not trusting this "stranger" to handle cash, pulled Levi, one of the younger volunteers, out of the sorting room and partnered him with Edwin.

Levi was home from college and had come down to the church to watch his sister in the play. Before he knew it he was thrust into the sorting room. He didn't recognize Edwin either.

"It's pretty amazing, you know," Levi said. "Watching all these people just hop to it when something needed to be done. Never seen nothing like it."

"It sure is something," Edwin said.

Levi and Edwin sold a ticket to nearly everyone outside the church and to many of the volunteers as well. If someone said they wanted to go, but didn't have the $2, Edwin put the money in the envelope on their behalf.

"You don't have to do that, you know," Levi said. "Pastor Isakson would understand. He'd let them in."

"It's OK, its just a few bucks."

"If you say so," Levi said. "You're a generous guy, that's for sure."

* * *

The play started 10 minutes late as the volunteers from the basement rooms finished up their last remaining projects and made their way upstairs. Large groups of friends and family moved from their assigned chores to the sanctuary. They filed into the sanctuary with moms and dads and happy children trailing behind them. It was a good place to be.

Everyone squeezed over into uncomfortably tight positions on the pews to make room for all the people. A fire marshal stood in the balcony, sucking on a candy cane. He crossed his arms and frowned. The place was certainly overcapacity, but he wasn't going to be the one to put a stop to this special night.

Edwin and Levi stood against the windows on the south wall. They had sold all 300 or so tickets on the roll, which should have brought in $600. Yet, they handed over nearly $1,000 in proceeds to the church volunteer.

"You sold 500 tickets?" she said.

Edwin explained that some people just gave them $5 or $10, but didn't ask for change, or just happily handed it over and didn't request a ticket.

"Sounds about right, I knew you weren't that good of a salesman," she said, with a smile. Maybe she did know he was from Mr. Z's. She handed him and Levi candy canes to reward their work.

When the lights finally dimmed, Pastor Isakson mounted the stage. The pastor shielded his eyes from the spotlight that was shining on him. He wiped a bead of sweat from his brow.

He thanked everyone for coming and discussed the surprisingly large turn-out for their little event. He only mentioned the camera once, but it made everyone in the audience turn and stare. This play was suddenly a very big deal.

"There's one man I'd like to thank for tonight above all others," Pastor Isakson said. "Well, not all others. Can't forget about the Lord. But there's another man who was inspired by the season to give. And he gave a lot tonight. If not for him, most of you wouldn't be here tonight. Let's give a big St. Mark's thank you and round of applause to Edwin Klein, owner of Mr. Z's toy store, for his generous donations to the children of this church."

Pastor Isakson pointed to the South wall and the young man operating the spotlight followed his direction until the spotlight landed on Edwin.

"I guess you are a generous man," Levi whispered. "You should have told me you were famous."

"I'm not famous, Levi," Edwin said. "Far from it."

"After today, I'm wouldn't be so sure about that."

Pastor Isakson told the assembled audience about Edwin's idea for a sale to donate to the kids; and how he and everyone else were shocked when Edwin donated his entire store, asking for nothing in return.

The applause was deafening. Edwin wanted to shrink away but he was sure that the spotlight would just follow him. Levi patted him on the back.

"You did a good thing, man," he said. "You should be happy."

"Thanks, Levi."

Pastor Isakson didn't say anything about Mr. Z's going out of business. Edwin wished he would have. It had only been a few hours, but he was already tired of telling people that the store was closed. The wound was fresh and it would remain that way for a long time.

After what seemed like an eternity, the spotlight returned to the stage and the play began. Mary and Joseph trotted onto the stage and battled it out with the innkeeper and various animals to eventually bring baby Jesus into the world under the watchful eyes of solemn wise men. Baby Jesus was not tossed into the air at all. In fact, the little play, which lasted all of 11 minutes, was quite good.

He wondered why the children and Pastor Isakson put so much time and energy into the play that was intended to be viewed by only a few people? And then, as the play came to a close and the children took their bows in front of the stage, Edwin knew exactly why they did the play. The pride that exuded from each and every child made it clear. They were actors and had helped tell a miraculous story.

Edwin was blind to the fact that he was now the original actor in a new Christmas story that would be told for years to come. The crowd cheered as the children grinned from ear to ear. Only then did baby Jesus get tossed into the air. Thankfully Mary caught him before Joseph could toss the little Savior again.

Thirty-One

Edwin, trying to avoid the mob of people who wanted to talk with him, snuck out of the sanctuary before the crowd streamed out of the church. He found himself in the gift room, surrounded by piles and piles of packages wrapped in red, green and silver paper. Taped to the side of each package was a label that indicated what sort of gift was inside—not the contents, but who the gift should be given to. At a glance Edwin could see that a particular package was intended for a girl between 12 and 14 years old who liked sports. Another package was for a boy age 3-5 who liked animals. Edwin marveled at how quickly the volunteers came up with such an efficient system.

A voice from behind Edwin startled him.

"I need your help," Pastor Isakson said. "We need to hand out these gifts, but most of the volunteers have already gone home."

"But there are thousands of gifts here and only a dozen kids," Edwin said.

"And we already gave out a bunch before the play started."

"What are you going to do with all the extra gifts?" Edwin asked.

"You tell me, toy man," the pastor said. "This was your idea."

"Double up on the kids in the play?" Edwin suggested.

"More like triple, and include their siblings too."

"Let's do it," Edwin said.

One by one the kids and their families were invited down to the present room where Pastor Isakson and Edwin would find just the right gifts for the kids.

"Thank you for doing this," said a mother of two. "We've had it bad this year and I lost my job in September. If not for you all, our Christmas would have been pretty rough."

"You're very welcome," Edwin repeatedly said.

When the last family came down and left with more gifts than they ever imagined, it became clear that giving out gifts like this wouldn't work.

"There are just too many presents left and now all the kids are gone," Edwin said.

"I've got one more idea," Pastor Isakson said. "But we need to get a move on, or the kids will already be asleep."

The two men loaded as many of the remaining gifts as they could into the church van that usually hauls food for Meals on Wheels. When the van couldn't hold any more, they drove to the Union Gospel Mission's Crisis Shelter for Women and Children. The shelter averaged about 70 women and children every night. Around the cold winter months those numbers rose.

Pastor Isakson went in alone and brought out the shelter's director, showing him the haul of gifts inside the van.

"We don't have time to hand them out, but if we leave them here, can you see that they go to the right kids?"

"You bet we can," he said with a smile.

They unloaded the van with the help of some of the residents, then drove back to the church for the remaining presents.

"You're a modern-day Santa Claus," Pastor Isakson said after they loaded the van again and drove to their next stop, the Salvation Army.

"I just picked the right day to go out of business, I guess," Edwin said.

The Salvation Army representatives were thrilled to accept the donations and emptied out the rest of the van.

"We saw you on the news," said one of the employees. "Thanks for thinking of our kids too. It's appreciated."

Edwin expected a firm handshake as a thank you for the gifts. Instead he received several big hugs.

"Hugs are more effective," one of the employees said. "We're all huggers."

"I'll have to remember that," Edwin said with a smile.

* * *

The men climbed back into the van, heading for the church.

"So what are your plans for the holiday?" Pastor Isakson asked.

"Honestly, I hadn't really thought about it yet," Edwin said. He had planned to spend the holiday with Amelia and the kids, but that was obviously out of the question since she had effectively vanished without a trace.

"You should come to the morning service," Pastor Isakson said. "I don't know if you're a religious man and I'm not about to give you a sermon tonight, because you've done enough good in the last six hours to save you from that fate. But I will tell you this. I saw you in a bad spot just a few weeks ago, drunk as a skunk."

If the van hadn't been so dark, Pastor Isakson would have seen Edwin blush with that comment. He recalled vomiting into a bucket in the same sanctuary, where the play was held.

"But today, I see a man at peace," Pastor Isakson continued. "I don't know what has brought about this peace, but you've got it and you need to hold onto it."

"I'll think about it," Edwin said, as they pulled up into the church parking lot and got out of the van. He had no intention of attending the service, but he appreciated the offer. "I haven't gotten much sleep lately. I have a feeling that when I get home, I might not wake up until New Year's."

Edwin wasn't sure what the pastor meant about being a man at peace. If losing your business in front of the country made him that, then he'd rather not find peace too often.

"Get your sleep. I understand that for sure," Pastor Isakson said. "You don't have a car here, do you? Hop back in and I'll give you a lift back to the store."

"No, that's OK, I think I'd rather just walk."

Pastor Isakson didn't hesitate to give Edwin a hug and a pat on the back. Edwin accepted the hug gratefully and then set off toward Mr. Z's and wherever he'd parked his car.

Just days ago he was decorating the front windows at Mr. Z's and planning for a big comeback. Now the window display was the only thing still intact at the store. It was Christmas Eve and he wanted to see the windows again. Not because he'd done such a great job on them.

Truth be told, he wasn't very good at it. But he wanted to see the memory that Mary envisioned. Their little apartment with two trees would live on in his mind. He picked up the pace as he turned onto Howard Street, but as he was just about the cross the street, a white van blocked his path.

Pastor Isakson rolled down the window.

"Apparently I just can't leave you alone tonight," he said.

"Apparently so," Edwin said. "What's up?"

"I had a feeling you might want this call right away. Remember what I said about finding peace and holding on to it?"

"Yes."

"I think peace just left you a message."

Thirty-Two

Edwin sat on his living room sofa balancing a half-cooked frozen dinner in one hand. As was his habit, he turned on the TV and watched as he ate. He nearly dropped his dinner when he saw himself staring back at him as dozens and dozens of people hugged him inside Mr. Z's. It was surreal watching the story play out on TV after living through it.

"This toy store owner, fed up with just scraping by, decided tonight on Christmas Eve, to donate every last remaining item in his store to kids in need," the anchor said from some studio in Atlanta. "It raised quite a stir in Spokane, didn't it Jean?"

They cut away to a reporter standing outside Mr. Z's.

"It sure did Kimberley . . ." the reporter began.

Edwin couldn't watch. He turned off the TV and set the frozen dinner on the coffee table on top of a stack of bills.

He turned his attention to the folded piece of paper that Pastor Isakson had given him. He'd read it a dozen times already, but he wasn't sure what to do about it. Or more accurately, he wasn't sure how he felt about what he planned to do about it.

The note, taken down by a receptionist at the church, just said, "Lost cell phone. Saw you on TV. Emergency with sister in Bonners Ferry. Had to leave. So sorry. Please call. Amelia."

Pastor Isakson said the receptionist had fielded dozens of calls from people who wanted to help the kids and the church and had started piling them up. But he saw this note in the pile and knew Edwin would want to know about it right away.

Edwin wanted to call but, it was so late now, he didn't want to wake Marcus and Susanna, especially if they were staying with Amelia's sister in Idaho. He stared at the phone and waited, but not long. He grabbed the phone and dialed. She answered on the first ring.

* * *

Barely two minutes after he hung up the phone, it rang again. Expecting it to be Amelia telling him something that she'd forgotten during their 10-minute conversation, he picked it up on the second ring. But instead of Amelia's sweet voice, it was an older man.

"I'm sorry to call you so late, Mr. Klein, but I wanted to get to you before anyone else did," the man said. His words were quiet but excited.

Edwin looked at the clock—10:45 p.m. on Christmas Eve.

"If you're telemarketing, this is really a bad time for it," Edwin said, a bit perturbed.

"Oh, no," the man said. "It's nothing like that at all. My name is Walt Riddell of Riddell Industries."

The way he said it, it was clear the man expected Edwin to recognize the name. Edwin had never heard of Riddell Industries before and thus remained silent, but also very close to simply hanging up the phone. What sort of person calls at this hour, anyway?

Walt continued.

"I saw you on television tonight. Heck, the whole country saw you tonight. You made quite the impression," he said.

"Failure will do that," Edwin said.

"I don't see it that way at all, not one bit. You've done something that has the very real chance of growing into a legend. A legend that will be retold each holiday season for many years to come. Something that has real staying power. It's a beautiful and tragic story."

"I appreciate your kind words," Edwin said, "but I'm afraid that this legend began and ended today. Mr. Z's is closed and that's a fact."

"I certainly hope that's not the case, Mr. Klein. In fact, that's why I called you at this awful hour. Give me five minutes of your time and if you're not interested, I'll never contact you again."

Edwin chuckled at the desperate pitch, but decided to play along.

"OK, Walt, you've got five minutes."

Walt made the most of his five minutes. In a seasoned voice he methodically laid out his proposal for Mr. Z's and offered Edwin something he'd dismissed just hours earlier. Hope. By the end of the conversation, Edwin's mind had shifted from pity and failure to guarded optimism for the future. Maybe it wasn't over yet.

Edwin fired up his computer while he was still on the phone and did a quick search on Walt Riddell and Riddell Industries. What he found looked very good.

As promised, when he checked his email there was a contract from Riddell Industries waiting for him. Walt had already explained the details, but Edwin had to be sure. His sleepy eyes pored over the fine print, but he found nothing to scare him away.

He provided an electronic signature, returned the contract immediately and closed his email.

It just seemed too good to be true. He couldn't wait to tell Amelia what had happened.

Thirty-Three

Bonners Ferry, Idaho

Amelia ran her fingernail across the single-pane window glass in the converted attic of her sister's small home in Bonners Ferry, Idaho. She watched a ribbon of frost flake off and disappear into the darkness that surrounded her. It was Christmas morning and, to her surprise, she was the first one awake. Or at least the first one she could tell was awake. She continued to lie in the bed, but she couldn't go back to sleep. Susanna was still sound asleep in the bed next to her. Not having a clock in the room, she imagined it was 5 a.m., but it was still pitch black outside. She was thinking of Edwin and the short conversation they had the previous night. He wasn't mad that she had abandoned him for the last two days, as she thought he might have been. They had a lot to talk about, but agreed to have that conversation in person.

Despite the short and pointed ceiling of the drafty attic, Amelia had slept very soundly. Besides, it was her old room and it felt like home. Her feet and back ached. Hustling for tips for two days at her sister's diner would do that.

Three days prior, Amelia was lying awake in her apartment in Spokane, going over the wonderful night she'd just had with Edwin and the kids at the hockey game, when her cell phone rang. At first she thought it might be Edwin, having changed his mind about staying the night with her. She happily answered the phone, but was surprised to hear the worried voice of her sister Amy. Amelia needed to come home.

Amy Cook was eight years Amelia's senior. She, along with her teenage son Max and pre-teen daughter Priscilla lived in the old house that Amelia and Amy grew up in. As tended to be the family tradition, both fathers of Amy's kids didn't stick around to fulfill their parenting obligations. Max was a muscle-bound tank of a young man, while Priscilla, was an artist, at least in her own mind.

Amy owned the town's only diner, aptly named Main Street Diner. She'd worked as a waitress, cook and manager at the place since she was 16 years old. Each week she'd save a portion of her tips and wages and deposit them into a bank account, never to be touched. It was a sacrifice for such a young person to make, but Amy never told a soul what she was doing. Every week her account grew—if only a little. After she graduated high school and worked at the diner full time, her nest egg grew even more rapidly. She bought some long-term CDs from the bank and started to earn interest on her nest egg.

She had never made a decision about what she was going to do with the money, which amounted to a little less than $25,000 when she turned 26 years old. When little Max arrived, she worked up until the day she delivered. She took two weeks off and intended to return to the diner, but Max's arrival coincided with the surprise retirement of the diner's owner, Rod Butler. The Main Street Diner was closing. Amy saw this as an opportunity to finally leave the town and take Max somewhere exciting like Las Vegas or Miami to set up a new life. She walked straight to the bank and requested to close her account and withdraw the savings she'd collected. But the bank could only give her $1,500, as the rest of the funds were tied up in CDs. She could withdraw the money, but would face a high percentage penalty, that would have erased any interest the funds had earned. She couldn't lose that interest.

For her, $1,500 was not enough money for a single mother to start a new life in another city. At least not the kind of life Amy wanted for her and her new son. She wanted more than a family that had to live week-to-week, paycheck-to-paycheck, just barely scraping by with an hourly wage. She didn't have an education or any skills that could easily transfer to something else.

And then there was her little sister Amelia who was just 15 years old then and already being chased around by high school boys. She worried that Amelia would get knocked up the first chance she got. Their mom had done them no favors. She worked as a part-time secretary at a lumber mill and spent more time screwing the mill's owner and trying to score crystal meth than parenting or even seeing her two daughters.

Amy's decision was easy. She couldn't take Amelia with her, but she couldn't leave her in Bonners Ferry to fend for herself either. Amy would not let Amelia end up like their mom. So she hatched a plan with Rod, the owner of the diner. He owned the building free and clear and hadn't even considered selling the business. Who would want to buy a lousy little dinner in far North Idaho, he asked? Well, she did.

For a down payment of $1,500 and the promise of continued payments as her CDs matured, Amy became the new owner of Main Street Diner. She was able to take her only known skills and turn them into a business of her own. Once she got an understanding of how the business and accounting worked, she realized that she didn't need to dip into her savings at all to pay Rod. She tightened up the diner's procurement practices and modified the menu so that more items could be made from the same basic ingredients. New management brought in new customers as well. It took five years, but she now owned the diner outright.

Amelia worked as a waitress for the diner from the day Amy made the arrangement to buy it. Despite Amy's constant warnings, Amelia just didn't have the ability to save like Amy did. They would go toe-to-toe about what Amelia was spending her money on—boys, clothes, make-up and whatever else she could waste it on. Saving it wasn't in the picture.

When Amelia became pregnant with Marcus, Max was already in kindergarten and Priscilla was still in diapers. The two sisters, with kids in tow, ran the diner like a military operation. No waste. All business. If something needed repair, they would first study and try to do the work themselves. Most of the time that strategy worked. In doing so, they both became rather handy to have around. They even used those skills to repair and remodel their mother's house that was about to go into foreclosure. Amy bought the house when their mom passed away.

They continued to live together in the house, even as the final member of their family Susanna arrived. The Cook sisters looked out for each other, although it was clear that Amy was the responsible one. She disliked and distrusted Josh—Amelia's boyfriend and the father of her children—from the minute she met him. He was too good looking to still be in Bonners Ferry. His long, wavy black hair was always perfectly coifed. He bought his clothes on the Internet so he didn't look like everyone else who shopped at the Big-Mart. It seemed cliché that he and Amelia would still be together. Josh was the high school quarterback who could have any girl. Amelia was gorgeous and an obvious target for him. She was content to settle on him and that infuriated Amy.

When Josh decided to attend the electric lineman school in Spokane and take Amelia and the kids with him, Amy protested. Loudly. While she refrained from bringing it up for fear of hurting Amelia, she was right about him. Josh left Amelia high and dry in Spokane when he moved to Reno and found someone new.

But Amy didn't have anyone of her own either, so Amelia wasn't too keen on following her sister's love advice.

* * *

Three days earlier, Amy was hauling trash to the dumpster in the back of the diner. Thanks to the snow, she didn't see the slightly raised concrete slab where the trash receptacle sat. She stepped halfway on it while reaching up to lift the trash bag. Her ankle rolled and something inside her lower leg snapped. She fractured her fibula where it meets the ankle. The break didn't require surgery, but she was placed in a cast and boot and told to stay off it.

The diner's business had expanded to more than just serving meals in the restaurant. They also provided catering services and were booked solid through the holidays with parties and family events. If she couldn't work they'd have to cancel all the catering jobs, which might as well be a death sentence for their business expansion. So, she called Amelia for help.

Amelia first protested that she had a commitment in Spokane. She'd met someone and he needed her, but after just a few minutes, she agreed to pack up the kids and drive north to Bonners Ferry. She couldn't tell Amy no.

Thirty-Four

Amelia slipped out from under the covers, careful not to wake Susanna, who had rolled toward the middle of the bed and right up against her during the night. Being in her old room again was an uncomfortable blast from the recent past. Yet more than that, being back in Bonners Ferry in her old job, serving the same customers as she had for years, was uncomfortable.

She'd received her fair share of, "we knew you'd be back," mixed with "nice to see you again, dear," from well-intentioned customers. Two days at the diner was enough to remind her of why she left. That life was not for her. She wanted more. Today was Christmas and thankfully the diner was closed.

Amelia dressed in a pair of black yoga pants, an old Bonners Ferry High School T-shirt and a pink bathrobe. She crept out of the attic room, down the short hallway and descended the stairs to find Amy already in the kitchen. She had a cup of coffee in her hand.

"Just like old times, right?" Amy said.

"How so?" Amelia replied.

"We're the first ones up on Christmas morning."

"True, but mom's not upstairs passed out cold in her 'going out' clothes."

"Good times," Amy said with a sarcastic grin. "You still take all that crap in your coffee?"

"Cream and sugar aren't crap. It's flavor."

"Not coffee flavor."

"When I want to taste the coffee I'll let you know, but for now I just need the caffeine."

Amelia looked at the Christmas tree in the living room adjacent to the kitchen. A small bounty of presents surrounded the bottom of the tree. Luckily the presents "from Santa" that she had bought for Marcus and Susanna were already in the trunk of her car, so she didn't have to explain to the kids why she was carrying Santa's presents to their aunt's house. Of course, Marcus wasn't the concern. It was Susanna and her insistence on knowing every nook and cranny of their Spokane apartment that worried her. There was no place to hide the presents where Susanna wouldn't find them. So she took to keeping them in the trunk.

"How are your feet?" Amy asked.

"Same old blisters, but at least I didn't break one of them."

Amy was sporting the cast and boot on her broken lower leg.

"I can't bear weight on it for eight weeks, isn't that insane?" Amy said.

"What are you going to do at the diner?"

"Jessie is back from vacation in a few days. I think we can manage when she's back."

The sisters had not discussed the lengths to which Amelia would help at the diner, not that it mattered much. Amelia didn't have a job to go back to in Spokane and she would do whatever her sister needed. She owed her that much and probably more.

"Tell me about the guy," Amy said. "I was a bit surprised last night when you dropped the bomb on me about seeing someone. I mean, I know we're not in the same city anymore, but you could have told me."

"It's not like that," Amelia said. "It was pretty quick. I wasn't hiding him. We were just, you know, busy."

"I know all about busy," Amy said. "Busy still has a phone, doesn't she?"

Her phone. The morning Amy called, as she raced around the apartment trying to pack the kid's things into a couple suitcases, she placed her phone in the front breast pocket of her blouse. Unfortunately as she fought the battle of rat's nests in Susanna's curly hair, she bumped the phone out of her pocket and right into the toilet, killing it instantly.

She tried to dry it off with a hairdryer, but did little more than make the phone hot and sticky. She'd hoped it would dry out in a few hours, on its own, but it didn't.

Edwin's phone number was in her phone and only in her phone. She needed to call him and tell him she wouldn't be able to come into the store. He'd be upset, but once she'd explained the situation, she was sure he'd understand. She didn't have the chance. His number was unlisted and the phone at the store just went to voicemail. She'd have to call him after the store opened, but when she tried again it just rang. No answer.

It seemed silly to her, in this technological age, that she had no other way of contacting him. But then she saw him on television and called St. Mark's. She left her sister's home number and the number at the diner. She didn't want to leave him only one option to contact her.

When Edwin called last night, she explained where she was and why, apologizing for leaving him unexpectedly. In turn, he explained everything that had happened at the store. Most of it she already knew from watching the news coverage on Christmas Eve, but she let him explain it to her in his own words. He didn't seem happy about what had happened, just resigned to reality. She invited him up to Bonners Ferry for

Christmas and he'd agreed to come up sometime that morning.

She wasn't nervous at all to introduce Edwin to Amy. If anything, she was anticipating a sense of relief in letting someone, other than her kids, meet him and provide an opinion. And Amy wasn't short on opinions either. She'd never shied away from sharing her feelings about Josh and how she just needed to get over him, because it just wasn't ever going to happen. She could do better and all that. Amelia never wanted to hear it. But with Edwin, she had the distinct feeling that he and Amy would get along just fine.

Maybe it was because Edwin was slightly older than she—closer to Amy's age in fact. Amy always viewed Josh as a little kid, even though Amelia and he were the same age. She thought about how well Marcus was doing around Edwin. How having a man around, even for a little while, had made a difference in him. He'd actually held a conversation with her on the drive up, rather than burying himself in some video game. She couldn't, of course, fully attribute that to Edwin, but his influence hadn't hurt any.

But whatever the future held for them, she was determined to enjoy today, Christmas Day. As if on cue, Susanna burst into the kitchen.

"I want French toast!" she announced.

"That's the first thing you say on Christmas morning?" Amelia asked.

"I'm hungry."

"Too hungry to open presents?"

"But nobody else is awake."

The thought of whipping up a meal after the last few days in and out of the diner kitchen was too much for Amelia.

"How about cereal for now?"

Susanna shrugged her shoulders, completely forgetting her desire for French toast. She disappeared into the living room and plopped down under the tree. Amelia got the milk and a bowl for her cereal.

"Don't shake all the presents," Amy said.

"I didn't," said Susanna, who clearly had.

"I was watching you, you little monkey," Amy said. "Now, knock it off. Being good all year starts today for next year."

"A whole year?"

"Yes, a whole year."

Susanna sat down at the table to eat her cereal. Amy and Amelia had joined her and resumed drinking their coffee, when the doorbell rang.

Without a word Susanna jumped down from the table and sprinted toward the front door. Edwin was early, Amelia thought. That was a nice sign.

"Do not open that door until I get there, missy," Amelia called after her. But before Amelia could round the hallway, she heard the click of the latch and crack of the door as the weather stripping squeaked. That girl will never learn.

"Oh, daddy!" Susanna said. At least that's what Amelia thought she heard.

She rounded the corner as Susanna burst through the open screen door and jumped into the arms of a man in a red Santa Claus hat.

At his feet was a tower of wrapped presents. As he hugged her, he turned to the side and Amelia's heart skipped a beat.

It was Josh.

Thirty-Five

"Hey, babe," was all Josh said as he gave her a quick kiss on the cheek and pushed his way past her into the living room. His two-days of dark beard stubble was rough against her face, but comforting and familiar too. Amelia did not resist the kiss. He looked good, maybe a little fitter than last time, if that was possible. She watched his hands as he arranged the presents. He was smooth and precise. No wasted or uncertain movements. He was capable, strong. It didn't seem like the same Josh she knew. He was different. It was unsettling not being able to pinpoint the emotions bouncing around her body. Was it joy and excitement or worry and regret? She couldn't immediately decide.

Susanna, after repeatedly hugging her father, ran upstairs to wake Marcus, who was sleeping on the bottom bunk in his cousin Max's room.

Amelia and Josh had been clear on their custody arrangement. She had full custody of the kids, but would allow for scheduled visits and trips so long as they wouldn't interfere with school or important events. Josh had never once broken those promises to see the kids, but he'd also always arranged everything well in advance. This surprise visit was a first. They'd never involved a lawyer in making their schedule, but now Amelia was left to wonder if she should have. Dropping in and out of the kids lives unannounced wasn't right.

Amelia had reluctantly accepted their particular situation, but still yearned to have Josh around in whatever capacity she could. Now, they were under the same roof for the first time in over a year and all those confused feelings rushed back in. They had experienced so much together for so many years that for the past year when she was alone, Amelia had a hard time figuring out where she had started and where Josh had ended. He'd always been there. Late-night feedings. Diaper changes. School conferences. Family functions. Talks at the end of the day. Good times and bad. Yet they'd never gotten married. Never made it official. This was a mutual decision, she told herself, but she knew better. He wouldn't commit.

But being on her own this last year wasn't her choice at all. It was his. He left them in Spokane to "find himself" or whatever he called it. The hurt from that event was more than enough to stop her cold, if she ever thought of them being together again. If he expected to waltz in here with some gifts and pretend like nothing happened, then he was sorely mistaken, she thought. Despite all that, she rushed upstairs, changed her clothes and quickly applied a bit of make-up. It couldn't hurt, she thought.

Josh sat on the floor near the tree with both Susanna and Marcus next to him. He'd provided no explanation as to why he'd come to the house, or how he knew the family was in Bonners Ferry. The kids' smiles were a mile-wide when Amelia came back downstairs.

"What the hell is he doing here?" Amy whispered into Amelia's ear.

"I have no idea," Amelia said, pulling her sister into the kitchen and out of sight.

"You should tell him to scram. This is a family affair," Amy said.

"Oh my God, Amy. Really?" Amelia said, wondering how her sister could be so cruel. "He's the kids' father. I'm not telling him to leave."

"If you don't, I will," Amy said defiantly.

"You will do no such thing."

"You've still got a thing for this guy, don't you?"

"My personal feelings aren't at issue here."

"They're not?" Amy said.

"No, they are not. Josh is here for Christmas with the kids and despite the fact that I had no idea this was happening, I can't take that away from them. They need their father."

Amy just shrugged and sipped her coffee.

"I'm not letting him stay here, you know," Amy said.

"He's staying with his parents," Amelia said.

"He told you that?"

He had told her no such thing and Amy knew it.

"Yes," Amelia lied, "he did."

Amy rolled her eyes and used her crutches to maneuver into the living room where all four kids were stacking up their presents in piles around the tree.

"Hello, Amy," Josh said, pulling off the Santa hat and brushing his nearly shoulder-length hair out of his eyes.

He gave her an uncomfortable handshake, like they'd just met.

"Josh," was all Amy would say, nodding.

Amelia and Josh shared a knowing look that Amy didn't catch. They'd always been able to do that, but it didn't take much to notice that Amy wasn't happy about their Christmas visitor.

"Daddy, Merry Christmas!" Susanna said.

"Merry Christmas to you too," he said. "I've missed you so much. You're like a foot taller than the last time I saw you. Did you take growing pills or something?"

"Mommy made me eat my vegetables, even though I didn't like them."

"She's right about the veggies and it worked too," he lifted her up and tickled her belly button. She squealed with joy, half-heartedly pounding his arm to let her go. Once he let her down and she escaped, she quickly returned to his lap and pressed her head against his chest.

Marcus didn't have the same gleeful reaction to his father's appearance. He gave him a hug and chatted for a second about growing muscles, but then lost interest and sank onto the couch near his pile of presents.

Josh's appearance had no impact on Max and Priscilla who simply wanted to open their Christmas gifts. Josh handed out the gifts he'd brought and the living room was quickly engulfed in a flurry of torn wrapping paper and ribbon as each child ripped into the packages. When the last gift was unwrapped Josh cleared a path to Amelia, who was sitting on the piano bench across the room.

"There's one last present I'd like to give to you," Josh said, looking at Amelia. He pulled out a black jewelry box from his back pocket.

Amelia's eyes went wide. Was he proposing to her? She couldn't be sure because it had never happened before and she didn't know what to expect. But before Josh could say another word, Amy stepped in front of him, standing on one foot.

"Oh, no you don't," Amy said. "Not today. You've played with this poor girl's heart enough. Let's not make it worse."

"Amy, let him talk," Amelia said.

Undeterred by her harsh words, Josh gave Amy a playful wave of the hand so she would step aside. She did. He opened the small box and pulled out a gold necklace with a red ruby pendant. Amelia's face flushed with a mixture of relief and disappointment. It wasn't a proposal after all.

"This was my grandmother's necklace," he said. "She wore it when she was first married in the 1950s. It was a gift from her husband. Before she died she gave it to my mother, her daughter-in-law. My mother wants to make sure that it gets passed along again, but of course, Susanna is too young. I'd like you to have it as your own until it feels right to pass along to her."

He unclasped the necklace and reached around her neck to put it on her. His face was very close to her own. She could smell the coffee on his breath. The necklace was long enough that she could lift it with her hand and still view the ruby pendant, which was resting in a nest of gold prongs.

"Of course, I'll keep it for her," Amelia said.

"By God, man," Amy said. "I thought you were going to ask her to marry you. You scared the crap out of me."

Josh turned to Amelia.

"I'm sorry, I didn't even think about that—I mean, about how that would sound," he said, stumbling to find the appropriate words. "I just wanted you to know the necklace was special."

"It's OK," Amelia said. "The necklace is beautiful. Please thank your mother for us."

"You can thank her yourself, if you'd like," he said. "My parents want you and the kids to come over today for dinner."

Dinner with Josh's parents? Not exactly the relaxing day she'd hoped for. The last thing she wanted to do was endure the condescending comments that invariably came from a face-to-face meeting with Josh's father. Amy disapproved of Josh, but it was nothing compared to the contempt Amelia felt for Josh's parents. His mother was tolerable at times, but his father was a first-class jerk. Some of the worst moments of her life were spent mere feet from Mr. and Mrs. Martin, who seemed to have a knack for pointing out flaws and belittling those who they didn't deem worthy of their time.

Amelia was deemed unworthy back in high school and never rose from that status. She was certain she never would either. Frankly she was surprised Josh's mom had given her the necklace, given their relationship. But, of course, it was intended for Susanna. Amelia was just the temporary keeper.

"I think dinner at your parent's house sounds great," she said, her heart sinking just a little.

Thirty-Six

While Amy got all four kids situated at the kitchen table for breakfast, Amelia and Josh put on their coats and exited the back door of the house. They stood under the plywood awning that seemed to bow with the weight of the winter snow. Nearly three feet of snow was resting on the roof and much more was piled up around the house, yard and every open area for miles around. It was snowing again—big, sloppy flakes. The weather report had said to expect at least a foot of snow and by the looks of it that would be the minimum amount. Amelia loved a white Christmas, but not the road conditions and snow shoveling that came with it.

Josh brushed off two of the patio chairs, but Amelia didn't feel like sitting.

"Why are you here?" she asked.

"I came to see you and the kids," he said.

"How did you even know I was here?"

"You've been in this town long enough to know that the minute you started back at the diner, everyone in town knew you were here. Gossip is the cheapest form of advertising."

"You're supposed to be in Reno working," she said. "Did you lose your job?"

"No," Josh said, looking a bit hurt by the accusation. "It's actually going really well and my apprenticeship is on track. I'll move up the ladder pretty soon."

"That's great."

"I got a few days off and drove up to see you in Spokane," he said. "I spent the last few days trying to find you. You weren't at the apartment. You didn't answer your phone, and the restaurant said you'd quit a month ago to work at some toy store. I called one of my buddies up here and he said he heard you were back at the diner in Bonners Ferry. So, I drove up last night and stayed with my folks."

"But why are you here?" she asked again.

"Things have, well, changed for me and I think changed for us too."

"There is no 'us' Josh, you made that clear when you left."

"That's why I'm here," he said. "I was wrong to leave and I'm sorry."

"So you say now. Did you new girlfriend kick you out?"

"I split with her months ago after I realized that I couldn't stand to be without you and the kids."

"So what's your plan? You want us to follow you to another city where you can just change your mind and move on again? That's not going to happen."

"No, we should get married and make this real. It's different this time. I've changed."

Amelia ignored his half-hearted proposal because any man, who is really proposing, is going to have to do much better than that.

"I've changed too," she said, holding her hand out and catching the snow as it fell. "I met someone."

She broke her gaze with Josh and started to think of all the virtues Edwin possessed which made her attracted to him. He was kind and compassionate and made her feel like she was special. He was good to the kids and they liked him, even though they'd only known him for a month. There was still a lot she didn't know about him and that worried her. Was Edwin a rebound?

She wondered. Technically he was, but it didn't feel that way. Regardless, she only had one real relationship to rebound from. The one that had given her two children, but also incredible pain and loss. She thought Edwin might be more of a long-term thing, but she never expected Josh to come back either.

She could see the jealousy in Josh's eyes and a piece of her really liked seeing him squirm. She knew how it felt and was glad he could taste it too.

"Who is this guy?" he asked, trying to sound nonchalant.

"He owns his own business in Spokane," she said. She felt no need to tell him that Edwin no longer owned much of anything. "He's very successful."

"La-di-da for him," Josh said. "So where is Mr. Big Shot, then?"

"He's actually on his way here this morning," she said.

"I thought you were going to come to my parents' for dinner?"

Amelia had totally forgotten that Edwin was on the way when she agreed to go to dinner in the lion's den of the Martin's house. She couldn't very well invite him along. Talk about awkward. But she couldn't let Josh see her indecisive, not after talking about marriage.

"I guess this will make it a bit more interesting at dinner then," she said.

"You can't be serious about bringing this guy."

"Serious as frostbite," she said. "Now let's get inside before I have to test that theory. Your kids want to see you."

Thirty-Seven

Edwin pulled his car into the Cook family driveway slightly after noon. The roads were becoming impassable due to the heavy snow and it had taken him twice as long to get to Bonners Ferry as he'd planned. He'd been forced to drive 15 to 20 miles per hour below the speed limit to avoid sliding off the road. The flashing lights of the many vehicles that had not heeded this warning littered the ditches along Highway 95. The little car was not built for winter travel.

He parked behind a blue four-wheel drive truck and wished he had something like that to navigate the roads.

The small white house was just as Amelia had described it. Charming in a dilapidated sort of way that made you want to grab a paint brush and start sprucing it up. But, as she said, the outside mattered much less than the inside, where life happens.

The long drive up gave him plenty of time to ponder what his next move would be. He was excited about the opportunity presented to him by Walt Riddell. But he couldn't do it alone, he'd told Walt that. He needed help and he wanted it to be Amelia, if she'd agree to it. The anticipation of telling her was almost too much for him. He nearly called her before he left, but decided it was one of those things you should talk about in person. He'd spent so much of the past few years barely hanging on that the idea of a change was unreal. Welcome, but unreal at the same time.

He'd already ignored several phone calls from Lance Massey, who was undoubtedly ready to demolish the Mr. Z's building at a moment's notice. He smiled knowing that Massey would lose, but Edwin wasn't in a hurry to tell him. He could wait at least until after Christmas to learn the bad news. He imagined the man sitting alone by a fire in a cold and dark living room like Ebenezer Scrooge, wondering why the world had decided to take the day off. Massey's timetable was of no consequence to Edwin any longer.

As he walked to the front door he was filled with optimism. He couldn't wait to share his news with Amelia and the kids. He was hoping for a home-cooked meal, something he'd been sorely missing lately. More than anything, he wanted to spend some quality time with Amelia and find out where things were headed. Over the past few days he had missed seeing her face and her beautiful smile. He'd missed not having someone with him. But he wasn't kidding himself either; he missed her physical presence the same way any man would miss an attractive woman. He could admit it. He hadn't felt desire like this since he lost Mary.

He thought about Mary too on the long drive up. She'd been gone for over a year, but not a day went by that he didn't pick up the phone to call her or think about what they'd talk about when he got home at night. She was just as much a part of him now as she was when she was alive, except she wasn't. She would be excited about the Riddell Industries deal. He wished he could talk to her about it.

* * *

When he knocked on the door to the Cook house, his anticipation level was at an all-time high. The door opened, but it wasn't Amelia standing there. It was some man with long hair and a firm jaw-line.

"I'm Josh," he said, sticking out his hand.

Edwin knew immediately who Josh was, but didn't even have time to offer his hand to shake as Susanna burst out of the door and wrapped her arms around his legs, taking both of them down into a pile of snow beside the walkway.

"Edwin! I win too!" she laughed.

* * *

Edwin accepted a cup of eggnog that Amelia had quietly noted was alcohol-free. He sipped at the vile drink and pretended to enjoy it. In truth, he'd rather be drinking toilet water than this odd creation that for some reason surfaced each holiday season. Yet his host, Amelia's sister Amy, had made quite a show about her homemade concoction that he wasn't about to refuse it. It was entirely possible that Amy had decided she needed to brew up a batch of the stuff just to stay out of the living room where he and Josh were left to their own devices. Amelia too had found some task that needed accomplished right away and exited the room after handing him the disgusting eggnog.

Josh, who clearly had much more experience in this area, explained the situation.

"They do that," he said.

"Do what?" Edwin asked.

"Busy themselves when something is uncomfortable."

"What's to be uncomfortable about?" Edwin said with a shrug of his shoulders that conveyed the situation in a way that they knew plainly and didn't need to belabor. There was no need to rehash what was obvious to both men. They were vying for the attention of the same woman and didn't know the other was in the running until today. Josh didn't know where he stood with Amelia, but he wasn't conceding just because Edwin had shown up.

"This stuff tastes like shoes," Josh said.

Edwin nodded.

"I thought I was the only one who thought that," Edwin said.

"Not by a long shot," Josh said. "She's never made this before, at least not that I can remember."

"You've known Amelia and Amy a long time then?" Edwin asked out of honest curiosity. He knew nothing more about Josh than a few details Amelia had mentioned.

"Yeah, since we were kids. Amelia and I went to school together every year since we were in third grade. My parents still live here in town too, only about three blocks away. It's a lot nicer around here than the desert in Reno, let me tell you."

"North Idaho's got a lot to offer," Edwin said. "I used to come up to Priest Lake in the summers. There was this little state-run campground called Indian Creek that my friend's family would camp at a couple weekends every year. We'd bring up the horses and ride the trails. It was really the best way to see the lake, unless you wanted to hike all day, which I wasn't interested in. My friend's dad was a hunter so I got to ride the trails in the fall and early winter too."

The two men talked for a long while about horses and riding, which Josh knew nothing about and Edwin was more than happy to share. It was a surprisingly easy flow of conversation and they bounced around to sports and weather. But they steered clear of the one topic they both knew was on their minds—Amelia. It wasn't the time.

Josh found the TV remote and turned on a basketball game that neither of them cared too much to watch, but focused intently on the action. Before long both men had fallen asleep in their chairs.

* * *

Someone in the kitchen dropped a pan, which startled Edwin from his brief and unexpected nap. Amelia peeked out from the doorway. Josh was still sound asleep, his snoring blocking out the announcers on the basketball game. Edwin was surprised to see it was already dark outside.

Amelia motioned for Edwin to follow her into the kitchen, where they sat at the table. Amy had taken Susanna and Priscilla into one of the bedrooms to play a board game. Marcus and Max were nowhere to be found.

It was Edwin who spoke first. He didn't want to dump his Riddell Industries news on her, not now. Not with Josh at the house. He wanted the chance to fully explain everything and feared he wouldn't get the chance today.

"I'm a third wheel—or maybe a fourth wheel on something that needs more wheels. No, less wheels," he rambled. "A wheel you don't need."

"Stop talking about wheels," she said, exasperated.

"I think I should just head out," he said. "If I leave now, I can be home before it's too late."

"No, I want you to stay," she said. "This isn't exactly what I'd pictured today, but I think we can make the best of it anyway. Besides, you and Josh seem to get along just fine."

What did she expect, he thought. That the men would come to blows? The mere fact that they hadn't didn't mean they were friends of any sort. In Edwin's brief estimation, Josh seemed like a pretty good guy on the surface. The kids loved him. But any man who would abandon his family had to have issues. He thought of his own father who he hadn't seen in decades. You couldn't trust a man who would leave his family.

"I just think it might be easier if I just go," he said. "You can enjoy the holiday with your sister and we can reconnect when you get back to Spokane. There's a lot I need to talk to you about. Big things."

"I like the sound of that, but even if I wanted to let you leave—which I don't—have you looked outside recently? There's already six inches of new snow on your car. There's no way that little sedan is going to make it down the block let alone to the highway."

Edwin turned and looked out the window. She was right. The entire car was buried.

"How long was I asleep?"

"Not long. The snow up here comes in waves and this storm looks pretty bad."

"So, I'm trapped here?" he said.

She gave him a look, but stood up from her kitchen chair and sat on his lap, wrapping her arms around his neck.

"Feeling trapped, huh?" she asked playfully and pulled him closer. She kissed him, but not a deep, passionate kiss. It was more of a tease that left him wanting more.

"More and more trapped by the minute," he said, as she nestled her face in his neck.

Thirty-Eight

Edwin finished losing his second game of Chutes and Ladders to Susanna when Amelia came into the living room. Susanna was thrilled with her victory and unaware that Edwin was letting her win each time. He figured the win meant more to her than learning how to play fair. Besides it was Christmas.

"Have you seen the boys?" Amelia asked.

"Not since before I took my little snooze," Edwin said sheepishly.

"We've got to get going to make it on time for dinner at the Martin's," she said. "Being late is a corporal offense."

Edwin had already insisted on not joining them for dinner at Josh's parents house. Amelia put up a mild protest, hoping that Edwin would provide a nice buffer to the uncomfortable evening. But she didn't want Edwin to feel any more out of place, either. He and Amy would have a simple dinner at the house with Max and Pricilla. He was pleased with the arrangement.

"They aren't here then," Amelia said. "I've looked everywhere."

Amelia hurried into the kitchen and Susanna followed as Josh put away the board game.

"Do you think they are over at Riley's house?" Amelia asked Amy. Riley was a neighbor boy and the same age as Marcus.

"They aren't there. I called," Amy said. "I called every parent I could think of. No one is home or they haven't seen them."

Amelia, normally at ease letting Marcus roam free, was anything but at ease and it wasn't just because they were due for dinner in 30 minutes.

"He knows better than to leave without telling me," she said. "Damn it, where could they be?"

Edwin came into the kitchen and heard Amelia curse, something he'd yet to hear her do. She was visibly upset at the boys' disappearance. He got an idea and walked toward the back door to confirm it.

"Do the boys have snowsuits?" he asked.

"Yes, they are drying on the hooks by the backdoor," Amelia said.

"No, they aren't."

Amelia pushed passed him to see for herself. The pants, coat, boots, gloves and hats that had been set out to dry from the day prior's outing into the snow were now gone.

"That means they are out there in the snow and not at someone's house," Amelia said, opening the backdoor with Edwin and walking outside, hoping to catch a glimpse of them building a fort or making a snowman. No such luck.

Edwin brushed the snow off the plastic thermometer nailed to the side of the house. It read 28 degrees. The wind was spitting snow vertically across the backyard. It was not the time to be out in the elements at all.

"I have to call Josh," she said.

* * *

Minutes later Josh arrived in his four-wheel drive pickup truck. Amelia was on the phone with the Sheriff's Department. They took a report, but said there wasn't a great deal they could do in such terrible weather and that the family had a better chance of finding them anyway since they knew where the boys liked to hang out.

"It's pretty typical for boys to run off for a few hours," the dispatcher told her. "That's what boys do."

"Not like this," Amelia insisted. "Not today."

She hung up the phone, infuriated.

"They won't help us find them. Let's go," Amelia said to Josh. She was dressed for Christmas dinner in a skirt and high heels.

"You expect to find them wearing that?" Josh said.

"I'll go," Edwin said, not waiting for Amelia's reply. "It'll be better for you to stay here if they call."

Amelia didn't want to sit idle, but didn't want to postpone the search either. Edwin was in clothes slightly more suited to be outside for a while so she relented.

"OK, just be careful and find them," she said. The desperation was evident in her voice. "My God, I can't believe I let him wander off."

"He's not alone," Josh said. "Max is with him, he'll protect him. It'll be alright."

"They are just boys!" she said. "They shouldn't be out in this."

"No, they shouldn't," Josh said. "But we'll find them. I promise."

* * *

Westmore Park sat adjacent to the First Baptist Church at the corner of Hayes and El Paso Street. The park with its large, wide hill devoid of trees had become a sledding haven for kids of all ages during the winter. The grooves and bumps in the hill under the snow made flying down a breathtaking experience. A set of stairs ran along the forested edge of the hill allowing kids to easily climb back to the top and careen down at full speed once again.

Josh pulled the truck in the parking lot and both men slogged through the snow to the base of the hill. A dozen or so kids, sleds in tow, were enjoying everything the hill had to offer. They waited at the bottom and asked several kids if they had seen Marcus or Max.

Josh felt a tinge of guilt in not knowing the names and faces of any of the kids. Bonners Ferry was small enough that it was reasonable to know every one of your child's friends, if not by name, then at least by face. None of them seemed familiar to him. Josh and the family had been away from the town for over a year and even if the family had still lived there, he doubted he'd have known any of the kids. That was Amelia's department.

While Josh waited at the bottom of the hill, Edwin walked to the stairs where a group of older kids stood. They hid their cigarettes behind their backs as he approached.

"Do any of you know Max Cook? He's an eighth-grader," Edwin said.

None of the boys replied, but continued to hold their hands behind their backs. Obviously not wanting to get caught smoking.

"Look, I couldn't care less about your smoking, I just need to find Max and his cousin Marcus. Do you guys know them or not?"

One of the boys took a long slow drag from his cigarette and blew a large white puff of smoke that dissipated in the air almost instantly.

"Max is friends with my little brother," one of the boys said. "What's it to you?"

"They've been missing for a few hours and we need to find them before this storm gets any worse," Edwin said.

"Sorry, man, I haven't seen him today. But it's not like we run in the same circles, you know? He's just a kid."

"How long have you been at the park?"

"I don't know. An hour, maybe."

"And you didn't see them during that time?"

"Nope."

Edwin wasn't sure how trustworthy the smokers were but, as they had no reason to lie to him, he took them at their word. He made it back to Josh, who had come to the same conclusion. The boys had not been at the park.

"They are on foot, so they couldn't have gone far," Josh said. "This just seemed like the most logical place for them to go."

"How far do you think they could have gone in two hours?" Edwin asked.

"In this weather, not far. But the streets are plowed, they could have walked almost anywhere in town."

"When you were a kid, is there anywhere else you would go and not tell any adults," Edwin asked.

Josh thought about it for a moment.

"Kampbell Cemetery."

"Is that close to here?"

"It's over the bridge, but it's worth a look."

The four-wheel drive truck had no trouble crossing the Kootenai River on Highway 95 toward the cemetery. Edwin had a hard time believing that the boys would have made the trip on their own, but Josh knew the town better than he did, so Edwin didn't argue. The cement barricades on the shoulder of the bridge were iced over from the blowing mist of the river. Every minute they drove made this path seem less and less likely to be one the boys would have taken.

The cemetery was surrounded by cobblestone pilings and black wrought-iron rails. The main gate was locked with a padlock. Josh shifted the truck into a low gear and punched the gas. The truck bounced up and down as they drove around the side of the cemetery taking a number of shrubs and bushes with them.

"There's a high spot around back," Josh said. "We'd hop the fence and then dig tunnels around in the deep snow over the graves. They never shoveled it, so it was perfect for goofing off."

Josh parked the truck and the men jumped out into waist-deep snow. It was obvious that the boys had not been to the cemetery. They'd never have made it through such deep snow.

Josh had to rock the truck back and forth, then drive it out backwards to get back to the main road. Josh's cell phone rang as they got back to the main road. It was Amelia.

"Irene Goodale said she saw Marcus and Max walking near Lincoln and Denver earlier today, before it got dark," Amelia said.

"That's right by the park," Josh said. "It's where we looked first."

For the next hour, they drove the streets at a crawl, looking for the two boys and calling out their names. No answer.

Since Amelia had failed to impress upon the county sheriff dispatcher the urgency of her need to find the boys, Amy decided to give it a shot by appealing to Sheriff Doug Washington personally.

"If you don't want the whole town to know why you drive to Sandpoint every weekend and return with a grin on your face, you'd better help organize a search party for my boy and his cousin," she said.

Sheriff Washington's wife would be none too pleased to discover the ungrateful slob, who slapped the waitresses' behinds at the diner, was keeping a mistress about 30 minutes south of Bonners Ferry in Sandpoint. If he was stupid enough to call her on his cell phone while he sat eating at the diner, then his deception was fair game, Amy thought.

In minutes the sheriff was on the phone with deputies on duty and called for a meeting at the Cook house. When Josh and Edwin arrived, they had to park down the street because of all the vehicles lined up in front of the house. It seemed as though everyone in town had come to help find the boys.

Sheriff Washington pinned a map of the town and surrounding area on a wall and directed Josh to highlight the roads and places they had already looked for the boys. Edwin hadn't yet seen a map of the area, but was surprised to see how little ground they had actually covered in the past few hours. The Sheriff then assigned each volunteer or deputy to search a select grid of streets. In minutes, the house emptied out as a dozen volunteers and deputies headed out into the night. Edwin stayed at the house, as Josh took his father, Marcus' grandfather, with him to continue searching.

"If this weather keeps up, I can't very well send people out there to look," Sheriff Washington said. "It's not safe."

"It's not safe for our boys either, sheriff," Amy said. "If they're out there, we have to find them."

"Yes, ma'am, but you have to understand my position," he said.

"I understand that you want to give up already and that's not going to happen," Amy said.

Edwin entered the room as Sheriff Washington stood to leave. Edwin had changed his clothes that had been soaked through from stomping through the snow. He had put on a dry pair of jeans and a flannel shirt. His tennis shoes, the only pair he brought with him, were dripping wet, so he walked out into the living room in just his socks.

"Hey, you're that toy guy from TV, right?" Sheriff Washington asked.

"Yeah, that's me," Edwin said.

"You're like a hero now," he said.

"I guess, but that's not really for me to decide," Edwin said. "At the moment, the only thing that matters is finding Marcus and Max."

"Sure, sure, but you're famous," the Sheriff said, putting on his hat to go. "That's pretty neat."

After he left, Amy retrieved a pair of hiking boots from the hallway closet and handed them to Edwin.

"These are better than wearing wet shoes," she said. "An old boyfriend left them here. I thought maybe he'd come back for them someday. Guess not."

They fit well. He was finally warming up, but would have much rather been wet and cold and looking for the boys. The three of them sat in silence in the living room, helpless to do anything to find the boys.

Edwin looked at the pile of discarded packaging and presents under the tree, including the doll that Marcus had stolen from Mr. Z's nearly a month earlier. He wondered what his life would be like today if Marcus hadn't been caught shoplifting. Edwin didn't like the image that came to mind. He thought of the booze and the lonely nights. So much had changed in such a short amount of time. He had a family to care about now and he would do anything to ensure they were safe. He felt Amelia and Amy's pain and worry and wanted to help end it. He needed to find the boys.

Still looking at the tree, Edwin saw something he hadn't noticed earlier in the day. Under a pile of cardboard, was a black polyester bag with the letters CCM stitched onto the side. CCM was a company that made hockey equipment. He picked up the bag and saw it was for hockey pucks. It was empty.

"Amelia, did you get Marcus hockey gear for Christmas?" Edwin asked.

"Yes, I got a hockey stick and pucks for each of the boys," she said. "They were sort of expensive, but it was what Marcus kept asking for."

Edwin couldn't believe nobody had thought of it earlier.

"I know where the boys are," he said.

Thirty-Nine

Edwin used a Sharpie and circled all the bodies of water on the map tacked to the wall. Marcus and Max had gone in search of a frozen pond or lake to use their new hockey sticks, he was certain of it. The hockey sticks were gone, as were the pucks that Amelia had bought them.

There were dozens of small ponds that were accessible by foot from the house.

"We did the same thing when we were kids," Edwin said. "Even without skates, playing on the ice makes it a lot more fun."

"And a lot more dangerous too," Amelia said.

One by one, they quickly discussed each small pond or lake trying to determine which would be the most suitable for playing on. They didn't seem to be any closer to narrowing down the right location.

Edwin was growing impatient.

"We're looking at this the wrong way," he said. "They wouldn't have had this discussion. They're just kids. They would have gone to the place they know best. One where they know how to get there by foot."

"You're right," Amy said, circling a lake east of the house. "Then it's got to be here at Rocktop Lake on Settler's Bluff. We hike that trail every week during the summer. It leads right to the lake. Well, it's not much of a lake. It's more like a pond."

"And Max would know how to get there on his own?" Edwin asked.

"Yes, so would Marcus," Amy replied.

"Does it freeze during the winter?" Edwin asked.

Neither Amelia nor Amy knew.

"I've never been up there during the winter," Amy said.

"Then what are we waiting for, let's drive up there and get them," Edwin said.

"You can't drive up there," Amelia said. "There's no road. It's only accessible by foot."

"What about a snowmobile?" Edwin asked. "That would be faster than trying to hike it."

"It's just a narrow little path, way too small for a snowmobile," Amelia replied. "It would have been a struggle even for them to walk up there."

Edwin looked out the window again out of the false hope that it had stopped snowing. By now a full ten inches of heavy snow had fallen since he'd arrived in town earlier that day. There was no way he or anyone else was going to be able to hike that trail on foot, which is probably why the boys never made it back down.

"I need you to find me a horse," he said.

* * *

Irene Goodale was already awake when she got the call. She'd been listening to the police scanner traffic and following along with the search for the boys. She was a regular at the Main Street Diner and had watched the Cook sisters grow up from girls into women. Max also did chores for her around the house during the summer. Since she was the last one to report seeing them, she felt responsible and wanted to help out. The widow was alone on Christmas and was more than happy to lend one of her two horses to Edwin.

Concerned that the Sheriff would call off the search altogether if they told him of their theory of where they boys were, Amelia and Edwin mutually came to the decision to not tell him about Rocktop Lake. Amy argued against it. It was a gamble, but if Edwin was wrong, neither of them wanted to pull resources from somewhere else.

Amelia introduced Edwin to Irene. He asked a series of questions about the horses, so he could get a sense of what conditions and terrain they were comfortable being ridden in and how they had been trained. Things didn't look good.

Irene had only ridden Hillary, the three-year-old filly, in pastures and on country roads. Taking an inexperienced horse, with an unfamiliar rider on a trail Edwin didn't know, wasn't going to be easy. Carter, a stallion that Irene said was 19 years old, was the other option. The dark brown horse was every day of those 19 years and maybe more. He lacked the muscle tone that Edwin would have liked to handle the ride, but he'd been ridden up the Rocktop trail many times before and was comfortable in the snow and cold.

It had to be Carter.

Edwin put on a rubber glove and smeared petroleum jelly under Carter's hooves and part way up his legs. The snow today was thick and wet, which was perfect for making snowballs, but also perfect for balling up and packing into the horse's hooves. Non-stick cooking spray would have worked just as well, but Edwin liked the thickness of the jelly. It was perfect for protecting the horse's legs.

Edwin hadn't been around horses for several years, but his skills were still sharp. Years and years of working with horses were hard to forget. It was as if he never stopped. The smell of the stables and the feel of the tack was like coming home to him. He was comfortable.

He placed the bridle into his jacket pocket to warm it up with his body heat as he groomed Carter. The grooming would help warm up Carter's muscles, something Edwin was concerned about given the horse's age.

"Why'd you put the bridle in your coat?" Amelia asked.

"I don't know this horse and he'll find any excuse to not do as I ask. Warming the bit gives him one less excuse," Edwin said.

Sure enough, Carter accepted the warmed bit without any hassle. Edwin led him out of the stable and into the bristling cold.

"The trailhead is four blocks from here, just past the firehouse," Amelia said. "You can't miss it."

"And the trail itself?"

"Carter knows where to go," Irene said. "He's not the fleetest of foot but he'll get you there."

Irene handed him a backpack.

"I figured you might need this," she said. "It's got some food, water and a first aid kit. I tossed in a few other things to keep you warm too. Now get a move on."

With that, she returned to the house leaving Amelia and Edwin alone by the stable. It was nearly 8 p.m. and the boys had been gone for at least five hours. If they'd been outside in these conditions this whole time, their chances of survival were slim. Edwin wasn't about to say that to Amelia, but by the look on her face, she knew the risks.

"If they're up there, I'll get them home," he said.

"Just be careful Edwin and call my cell if you find them," she said. "I'll be waiting at the firehouse at the trailhead when you come back down."

She paused.

"Wasn't there something you wanted to tell me?" she asked. "You said it was something big."

"Yes, there is something," Edwin said, "but it can wait until I get back."

She kissed him. Their cold noses were numb from the weather. Their faces were wet. The snow was coming down so hard that Edwin couldn't see more than 10 feet in front of him.

"Thank you for doing this," she said.

He smiled and gave her another kiss before mounting the horse.

"Thank me when I get back with the boys."

Forty

Had Carter not walked the trail before, Edwin was certain that he'd never have been able to stay on it. It was too dark and the snowdrifts obscured the way. The moon provided the only faint light, but it barely shone through the think canopy of branches overhead. The trail twisted and turned as it rose up Settler's Bluff. The trees were weighed down with snow and Edwin was dumped on several times by branches giving way. The snow wasn't as deep under the canopy, but it was still treacherous.

Edwin maintained Carter at a walk only. Even when a stretch of trail was clear, he avoided trotting the horse for fear of hitting ice or frozen leaves that could cause Carter to lose his footing. Such an event would be disastrous for both the horse and the rider. But Carter climbed the trail with no fear and obeyed Edwin's directions like they had been together for years. The seasoned horse was exceeding his expectations.

Had circumstances not forced Edwin out into the night, he would never have attempted this ride alone. The soft snow muted nearby sounds like a blanket, so much so that Edwin feared he might miss any cries for help or the sounds of an approaching animal that might see him as dinner. Irene had warned him to be wary of wolves that had been spotted in the nearby Kootenai National Forest. He only had her word to go by, but it was enough to keep him alert. He only carried a pocketknife, which wouldn't do much against an advancing pack of wolves.

Every two minutes he would pause briefly and call the boy's names. His voice seemed to get swallowed up by the night. No answer. He was alone.

As he approached a narrow clearing he could hear the sounds of a trickling stream, which was a bad sign for several reasons. First of all, the stream was probably coming from Rocktop Lake, which meant it wasn't frozen. The second reason this sound was upsetting was because Max and Marcus would have undoubtedly heard it too. The likelihood of them continuing on after seeing the stream trickling by them was slim. He began to question whether this trek up a mountainside, in what could easily be called a blizzard, was a wild goose chase. Did he want to impress Amelia so badly that he put himself in this position? Destined to fail again? He was trying to find a reason to turn around, but forced himself to continue.

Once through the clearing, the trail twisted to the left. Edwin pulled back on the reigns to listen. Carter's huffing breath was the only sound he could hear. He could see most of the town below him, and several headlights slowly snaking down its streets. They were still searching. They hadn't found them yet.

He pulled the hood of his coat tighter around his stocking cap, knowing it would further impede his hearing, but he was really starting to feel the chill in his core. He had considered riding up the mountain bareback so he could share the horse's body heat, but decided against it. He was concerned that if the boys were injured, they would need the stability of a saddle to ride back down.

To guard against losing the heat he'd taken one of the riding blankets and cut a hole in the middle, draping it over his legs and Carter's flank. It was a modest attempt that wasn't doing much good at all.

After another few turns, the trail in front of him split, a literal fork in the road. To the right was a steep climb, but on the left was the relatively smooth continuation of the trail. The stream sounds had come from the left, so Edwin elected to ride on the trail he'd been on even though the steep trail would likely reach the lake faster since it was at the top of the bluff. Neither trail looked to have any footprints. Again, a bad sign, yet with the drifting snow, it was nearly impossible to be sure.

He whistled for Carter to walk on to the left, but his commands were ignored. Again Edwin whistled, but this time gave the appropriate reigns a tug as well. Carter wouldn't budge.

Edwin dismounted the horse and tied a loose knot to a nearby sapling. He hit the ground with a crack. There was ice under the snow. How had he not heard it crunch before? If Carter slipped on the ice, it was all over for them both. He walked down the left trail about 30 yards, when he lost his footing and ended up landing hard on his side. The fall knocked the wind out of him. As he tried to stand he felt a piercing pain between his ribs on the right side. He'd broken a rib or two. No question. He tried to catch his breath, but could only take in short quick breaths as the pain in his ribs enveloped his upper body with each intake. He had to push through. He struggled to his feet.

The trail had simply disappeared. He tried to see where the trail resumed, but he couldn't make it out. The edge of the bluff had just washed away, which must be the reason the steep trail was added—out of necessity. When he got back to Carter, he gave him a gentle rub on his forehead.

"You really do know this trail, don't you?" he said.

He looked at his watch. He'd been walking for over 30 minutes by now and certainly at a faster pace than two boys could hike in his cold. He could feel the cold air being pulled into his lungs and the chill emanating throughout his body. He needed to find them and get off this mountainside fast or none of them were going to make it out alive.

He shouted in pain as he hoisted himself up onto the horse.

Carter pushed up the steep trail, which intersected with what Edwin assumed was the original trail after a short climb. As they moved onto the flatter trail, Edwin saw his first sign of hope. The snow on the ground was thin thanks to the tall pine trees that surrounded the intersecting trails. Scattered in the snow were unmistakable footprints. Edwin was no tracker, but snow had definitely been disturbed recently. Someone had been up here.

He couldn't resist pushing Carter to walk faster as he followed the footprints. After 10 more minutes of walking he made it to the lake, but lost sight of any more footprints.

* * *

Rocktop Lake was no more than an oversized pond. Edwin estimated that it couldn't be larger than two acres total. The thick tree line hugged the shore at every curve. Snow covered the entirety of the lake. The snow was heavy and Edwin couldn't tell where the beach ended and the water began. It was frozen after all.

He tied up Carter and called out for the boys again. This time he heard something in return.

"We're out here!" Max yelled. His voice was weak and distant.

Edwin retrieved a flashlight from his coat pocket and shined it toward the middle of the lake. The barrage of snowflakes was blinding. The light did him no good. He squinted and could just barely make out Max waving from what had to be an island in the middle of the water.

"You need to come to shore," Edwin yelled back. "I'll lead you out of here."

"I know, but Marcus won't cross the lake. He fell in and he is really cold!"

Edwin didn't think. He just acted. He removed a long rope from one of the saddlebags and double knotted it around a tree trunk. He tied the other end to his belt and stepped onto the ice, but his foot punched right through, soaking his right leg up to his calf. He jumped backward toward the shore. The lake wasn't completely frozen.

Still tied to the rope, Edwin searched for a dead tree to snap and use as a broom. He found a three-foot Evergreen missing all its needles. He kicked the trunk and split the tree instantly. Returning to the lake, he moved slightly to the right of where he'd broken the ice. He waved the branch to brush off the snow. He could see the different shades of white ice. The ice seemed to be thinnest at the edges, but thickened somewhat a few feet in. He used the branch and probed the ice in front of him. It seemed more solid, but there was really no way of knowing.

"Hurry!" Max yelled. "He's not talking anymore."

Edwin pulled the rope tight to use as leverage if he slipped. Placing one foot on solid ground, he slid his other foot out as far as he could. Leaning on the ropes, he brought his feet together. He was now standing on solid ice, but for how long? Slowly he inched toward the island, keeping the rope tight the entire time. He wasn't a big man, but he'd give anything to weigh 50 pounds less at that exact moment.

He continued this ritual of probing the ice and inching forward, listening for any signs that the ice might cave in. He made steady progress and could soon make out the outline of the island and Max standing at its edge.

Expecting the same thin ice surrounding the island as surrounded the shoreline, Edwin got onto this hands and knees, hoping to distribute his weight more evenly. As he crawled to the island as fast as he could. His heart was racing and his instincts told him to slow down, but he ignored the panic. Marcus needed him. He wasn't going to pass out, not now. Damn the heart defect.

He was close enough to the island that he didn't have to yell to be heard.

"How long since he went in?" Edwin asked, continuing to crawl.

"Like, 15 minutes ago, maybe," Max said. "We were just playing and then he was gone."

"He went all the way under?"

"No, just to his waist."

That wasn't much better. Edwin had seen hypothermia before. The body just slows down when shocked with the cold. If he'd been exposed for even five minutes, he could be in trouble, but 15? That was a very long time.

Edwin clasped Max's outstretched hand. The older boy heaved Edwin forward and the two landed side by side in the snow.

Marcus was curled up into a ball, leaning up against a tree. He had shirts on both legs. His wet pants sat in a frozen pile next to him.

"I had him take off his shirt and wrap it around his legs. I gave him my shirt too. I figured the coats could keep us warm," Max said.

"That was a good idea Max, but we need to warm him up with our body heat too," Edwin said.

Edwin took off Marcus' coat and put it on him backward so the zipper was open on his back. He then unzipped his own coat and pulled Marcus onto his lap, pressing their bodies together. It was the same theory he'd used with the horse blankets over him and the saddle—sharing body heat. He silently wished he had brought the blanket with him out to the island. It would have made this a great deal easier.

Marcus' eyes were open, but unfocused. His teeth were chattering, which Edwin thought might be a good thing. His body was still fighting the cold. The pressure of Marcus against his ribs was unbearable, but he hugged him tight.

He needed to raise his body temperature, but had nothing on him that could help. Then he remembered the backpack Irene had given him. He'd completely forgotten that he still had it on. Max pulled it off his back and dumped out the contents in front of him. A few bottles of water, energy bars, a red first aid kit and a flare gun spilled out. Edwin unzipped the first aid kit. Irene must have packed it just for them. Inside were four plastic sealed hand warmers that heat up when exposed to the air. Edwin ripped the plastic open and placed one under each of Marcus' armpits. He directed Max to stuff the other two inside Marcus' shoes. The little packets would do very little to help warm Marcus, but it was all they had.

Edwin didn't know if making him eat or drink would be beneficial or not, so he did neither.

Next, he examined the flare gun. If he could see the lights from the cars halfway up the bluff, it was likely that they would see the flare shot from the bluff. He inserted a cylindrical cartage and fired the gun into the air. Nothing happened. He tried again. Nothing. He opened up the chamber to remove the cartridge and noticed that the pin holding it in place was closed. He flicked it with his finger. In that exact moment, the gun fired, shooting a bright orange flare across the surface of the lake until it came to rest in a mound of snow neatly hidden from anyone who might need to see it. He looked for another cartridge, but came up empty. The flare gun was useless now.

Then he remembered. He had a cell phone.

Forty-One

Edwin patted his pockets, searching for the phone. He didn't have it. It was inside the saddlebag strapped to Carter. He had to be the worst rescuer in history, he thought. If he had the phone he could call for help at least. Maybe they could airlift Marcus out with a helicopter, but the wind was getting worse and he didn't know if helicopters could even fly in snow. He couldn't risk going back for the phone and leaving Marcus on the island alone. What if the ice broke and he couldn't get back to him? He had to take him along, but that would mean leaving Max behind.

He formulated a plan.

He removed his coat and immediately felt the blistering cold air knife through his body. He removed Marcus' wet shoes and shoved his legs through the arms of his jacket, zipped it and then tied it tightly around Marcus' waist with the cord in the bottom hem. He replaced the wet shoes and the hand warmers inside them. Marcus' calves were still exposed, but at least he was basically dry and still warming up.

The wind began to howl and he had to shout when he spoke to Max.

"Can you cross back over?" he asked.

"Yeah, I can do it," Max replied.

"OK, I'm going to hold the rope tight for you," he said. "Walk slowly and don't put your feet together. Distribute your weight. Follow the rope back. If the ice breaks, hold the rope. The ice should be solid along that path, except for the edge near the shore. Got it?"

"I think so."

"When you get to the other side, I want you to go to the horse and get my phone out of the saddlebag. Call 9-1-1 and tell them where we are and that we're going to head back down the bluff. They should send someone up the trail with something to warm Marcus because I think hypothermia has already set in. You got all that?"

"Got it," Max said.

"Remember to keep the rope under your arm, so if the ice cracks, you can just hang onto it."

Edwin didn't like sending Max back first, but in theory, it should work. Since Max was significantly lighter than himself, it was a safe play . . . he hoped.

Edwin pulled the rope tight. Max didn't pause once as he crossed the frozen lake. The path was solid, Edwin was certain now. Max walked to the horse and Edwin saw the flash of the cell phone light as he called 9-1-1. Now to get Marcus up and moving.

"Buddy, you've got to get on your feet," Edwin said, patting his cheeks.

His face was pale and cold.

"It's not that far Marcus, you've got to get up."

No response. He couldn't walk on his own. Edwin would have to carry him.

He looked for somewhere to tie to rope other than his own belt. The rope wasn't long enough to reach anything stable, so he tied the rope under Marcus' arms. He picked the boy up as his ribs and side seemed to catch fire. He tried to ignore the pain and draped Marcus over his shoulder in a fireman's carry. The adrenaline coursing though his body made the boy seem incredibly light.

He felt the rope tighten and knew Max had grabbed the other end to pull them in. Smart kid, he thought.

With small rhythmic steps Edwin walked triumphantly across the lake with Marcus over his shoulder. He took little breaths so his rib cage wouldn't expand and force the fire-like pain again. He could see Max at the end of the rope. He could see Carter, bucking his head waiting for them. Help was on the way. It was going to be all right. He'd saved the boys.

Then it happened.

He heard the ice crack just before he was submerged underwater in a split second. His eyes wouldn't open. Everything was black. He waved his arms to push Marcus up onto the ice, but Marcus was gone. He spun around under the water holding out his arms in search of the boy. Marcus wasn't there. He pushed his legs down and hit the sticky bottom of the muddy lake. The thrust propelled him to the surface and he stood up straight, his head just above the water. He sucked in a huge misty breath and everything started to slow down. His ribs didn't hurt anymore.

Had he been fully alert he would have recognized that his body was in shock. But he wasn't alert. He was far from it. He choked as he spit out a mouthful of icy lake water.

At the surface he saw feet in front of him getting smaller and smaller. His ears hurt. They were ringing. The feet were snaking away from him. Where were they going? He tried to grab for them, but his arm wouldn't rise above his shoulder. His hand hit something hard. What was it? He didn't care. He wanted to sleep. He closed his eyes as his knees buckled.

Something sharp hit his face and he again tried to grab for it. This time his hand broke through the ice. He reached forward as he was struck in the face again.

"Edwin!" Max shouted. "Grab the rope!"

Edwin finally became fully aware of what had happened. Max had pulled Marcus to the shore, then tossed the rope to him. That's what hit him in the face. Twice. He grabbed onto the rope, but it slipped out of his hands as Max tugged harder.

"Wrap it around your arm!" Max screamed.

Edwin did as he was told. Max leaned back with all his strength and pulled Edwin toward the shore, splitting the ice as he went. When Edwin was close to the shore and dragging along the bottom of the lake, Max dropped the rope and grabbed him by the armpits, pulling Edwin to the tree line.

"I did what you said," Max told him. "I called for help. They are coming."

Edwin nodded to Max.

"You did good," Edwin said quietly. "You saved your cousin."

Edwin stared at the sky from his back. He was warm, really warm. He watched the snow dance above him. It filtered down and spun to the ground. The white light was blinding. Headlights. He thought of the drive to the airport the night he lost Mary. It was snowing like this. It was good snow. He liked it. It felt nice.

He saw the toy store filled with happy customers. He saw Mary kneeling next to a little girl at the counter. It was the little girl Mary had lost at three months. Her brown hair was tied up into a ponytail. She looked just like her mom. She was a beautiful, miniature version of his wife. The girl waved at him as Mary smiled.

Edwin needed to go to them. Now.

"Don't wait for me," Edwin said to Max, but he couldn't see him. Not anymore. He was looking at something wonderful that Max and Marcus couldn't imagine. He could see Mary and the little girl in the white snowy headlights. They were calling for him.

"I can't leave you," Max said as tears welled up in his eyes, but Edwin didn't hear him. Not anymore.

Forty-Two

It was Josh who first spotted Carter ambling down the Rocktop trail. He and Sheriff Washington had been on the trail for only about 15 minutes. They had followed the horse's deep prints up toward the top.

When Marcus called 9-1-1, the dispatcher made the announcement on the same frequency so all of the searchers could hear. The boys were on Settler's Bluff at Rocktop Lake. They were headed down, but needed medical attention for one of them. Marcus had fallen through the ice.

Two heads bobbed up and down on Carter's back. Max and Marcus.

Josh pulled his son off the horse and wrapped him in a chemically heated blanket he'd retrieved from the firehouse at the trailhead. His face was blue, but he was breathing. Sheriff Washington offered the same blanket to Max, who steadfastly refused it.

"Where's Edwin?" Josh asked.

Max shook his head, tears streaking his face. "Gone."

"What do you mean, gone?" Josh asked.

Max just shook his head.

* * *

Marcus spent three days in the Boundary Community Hospital recovering from mild hypothermia and frostbite. But even when he was released, he was still on the mend physically and emotionally. It would take weeks to fully recover. The frostbite on his calves was the worst, but thanks to Edwin's coat that had been wrapped around his legs, the rest of him had avoided any lasting damage, at least on the outside.

When they'd gotten to the firehouse on Christmas night every member of the search party was there. Max made a beeline for his mom, Amy. He began to speak and didn't stop speaking until he had told her exactly what occurred that night. They had gone in search of the frozen lake and had played on the ice until it was too dark to see. When they decided it was finally time to head back, Marcus fell through.

He explained how Edwin had arrived shortly after Marcus went in the water. He had saved them. Had he not shown up when he did, Marcus wouldn't be alive. He had no doubt about it.

He told his mom that Edwin smiled at the end. He just went to sleep and he looked happy. He tried to wake him, but he couldn't. He would have stayed, but he needed to get his cousin to safety and Edwin told him to go. He told him not to wait for him. He had saved them because he said to go. He wanted them to leave.

Max cried in his mother's arms as the assembled search party watched and listened. He would never tell the story again, but he wouldn't have to. They all heard every word.

Forty-Three

Edwin's funeral was held at St. Mark's Church on New Years Eve. Amelia had made the arrangements with Pastor Isakson. The media had returned. The story was too big. Just one day prior to his death, they reported, Edwin Klein had escaped an armed robbery, donated his entire toy store to kids in need and taught the nation how to be selfless. Then he gave the most precious gift of all to save two young boys who were stranded on a frozen lake. Edwin Klein was already a legend.

Marcus sat in the front row of the church, sandwiched between his parents Amelia and Josh. Susanna leaned against her father. Beside her were Max, Amy and Priscilla. Max did his best to act tough, but he was hurting too. He had been offered the chance to stay home. He wouldn't hear of it. He owed Edwin. They all did.

Edwin's mother and stepfather had flown in from South Carolina and sat on the opposite side of the church aisle. Amelia had thrown her arms around Edwin's mother the moment she saw her. Amelia didn't say a word. She didn't have to. They both knew Edwin in their own way and they knew what he'd done for the boys. The two women embraced for a long while.

Pastor Isakson mounted the stage, which was still decorated for the Christmas play. He stood behind the podium. He knew Edwin wasn't much for religion, so he centered his brief eulogy on the virtues of giving and the strength of love.

He told the packed church a story they had never heard. It was one that Edwin had told him the night they drove to the women and children's shelter and the Salvation Army to donate the last remaining toys. It was the reason that Edwin wanted to give, because he'd received so much.

When Mary was just a teenager she worked at Mr. Z's nearly every day after school. During winter break she'd work from open until close. She would help customers or run the register. She'd stock shelves. Whatever needed to be done, she'd do it. But the one thing she was really good at was listening. Sure, there were bratty kids who would whine and cry that their parents wouldn't buy them some new toy for Christmas. But she would listen for the kids who were simply resigned to the fact that they wouldn't get what they wanted. Or couldn't buy what they wanted for someone on their list. Mary couldn't have that. Not on Christmas. One day she heard a boy talking to his mom about a set of plastic farm animals and a barn.

"But he needs to have his own stables, mom!" the little boy pleaded.

"Honey, I agree with you and he's taught you a lot," the mother replied, "but it's not our place. I appreciate your generosity, but I can't afford it. Not with the cost of your lessons."

Mary, eavesdropping from an aisle over didn't know what type of lessons the little boy was talking about and she of course didn't know who the gift was intended for, but what Mary had heard met her criteria perfectly. She rounded the corner and handed the boy a small gold card that read, "Any Item $1 With This Card." The boy thanked Mary, scooped the box off the shelf and ran to show his mom. Their eyes met and Mary nodded to say it was OK. The mom mouthed the words "thank you" and they never saw each other again.

"You see," Pastor Isakson said, "Mary never told anyone that she handed out these little gold cards or that she paid for the gifts out of her own pocket."

A decade or so later Mary was organizing her and Edwin's belongings in their first apartment. She needed to make room in the closet for something, when she discovered a familiar looking farm animal box with a gold card attached. A handmade card, attached to the outside of the box was addressed to Edwin. The card read "To Edwin, the best horse-riding instructor ever. Now you can have your own stable of horses too."

Pastor Isakson paused to ensure the audience made the connection.

"You see, some souls are just meant to find each other. Mary and Edwin are such souls," he said. "We can take solace in that today, the day we mourn our friend, Edwin Klein."

* * *

Amelia stood against the back wall of the church basement, cradling a cup of coffee that had been provided for the reception after the funeral. Amy and her kids had gone. Josh had taken Marcus back to the apartment. He still wasn't feeling well and Amelia thought it would be best for him to keep to himself as he worked through the feelings that had arisen from the night Edwin died. Susanna, across the room was as bubbly as ever, harassing Pastor Isakson about something or another. She was in good spirits, but she was too young to understand the complex emotions that the adults in her life were feeling.

Amelia herself was drawn. She hadn't been able to eat all week. She blamed herself for what happened. At every turn she could have ensured that Edwin wasn't in their lives. She forced herself onto him as an employee at Mr. Z's. She wanted a relationship. She invited him to Amy's house. She didn't watch Marcus closely enough and he nearly died because of it—Edwin actually did. She was a wreck.

The past week, Josh had been her rock like never before. He'd taken over much of the responsibilities with the kids as she dealt with her grief and guilt. He'd come to stay with them in Spokane. Who knew what would happen with them, but he was acting like the man she'd always wanted him to be. They both knew it. But she was still as low as she'd ever been.

Pastor Isakson appeared at her side.

"I've seen that look before," he said, not looking at her.

"What look?"

"Your look," he said. "The one on your face."

"I imagine you have. It's a funeral," she said, a bit more smug than she'd intended.

"No, no. Not that. Sure, people are sad. They should be. It's what we'd all like at our funeral, to know that people cared about us. But the look I'm thinking of wasn't from today. It was on our friend Edwin's face only a few weeks ago. He was in the dumps. Down and out."

Amelia remembered getting Pastor Isakson's call to pick up a drunk Edwin who had fallen asleep outside the church.

"That was pretty bad," she said.

"But, you see that's not the man I remember," he said. "I remember the man he was, not the sad memory. The man he was, was thanks to you."

"You can hardly say I had anything to—"

"Enough. I don't want to hear it," he said, holding up his hand. "You, my dear, helped the man find peace. I saw it. Sure, he met a tragic end, but when our time is up, it's up. There are no chance encounters. Not even little ones."

"It's a wonderful thought Pastor Isakson."

"The question you must ask yourself now is what will you do with what you've learned," he said.

"I'm not sure I know, yet," she said.

"You will. Trust me. You will."

* * *

Amelia retrieved her and Susanna's coats from the church's cloakroom. She bent down to button up Susanna's winter coat before finally heading out. The reception was still going strong, but it was full of people she didn't know and she just needed to escape.

They had just climbed the basement stairs and were headed down the long foyer to the exit when the front doors burst open. A man in a dark gray overcoat and black leather gloves stomped into the church and rushed passed them without a word.

When Amelia reached to door, she stopped suddenly as the man called out her name.

"Amelia Cook?" he asked, walking toward her while taking off his gloves and reaching out his hand.

"Yes, that's me."

"Oh, thank goodness I caught you. I thought I'd be too late. My apologies. My flight was delayed and I just now arrived in Spokane."

"And who are you?" Amelia asked of the elderly man with the soft voice.

"Forgive me. My name is Walter Riddell of Riddell Industries. You and I have a lot of catching up to do."

Forty-Four

November, one year later

Amelia sprayed and wiped down the inside of the store window for the fifth time that day. Mr. Z's display windows had never seen so much shine. She slowly stepped out of the scene, careful not to smudge the windows. She could hear Josh hammering away at something in the back room. He'd really taken to the project, but they were on a tight deadline to get everything ready for the next day when Mr. Riddell, or Walt as he insisted on being called, would be in town to inspect her first display window scene.

Her stomach was in knots. There were so many details to oversee, but it felt good and they were going to have a great showing.

On the previous Christmas Eve after a brief phone conversation with Walt, Edwin had signed a five-year, binding contract with Riddell Industries to preserve Mr. Z's in its current location and decor, but with the understanding that Riddell Industries would franchise the store in multiple cities. The franchise model would improve buying power and thus lower prices, but also maintain the sort of mom-and-pop establishment that had long been a tradition in Spokane. Walt knew Edwin's donation story would certainly be remembered, but only if capitalized on quickly.

Edwin had given Walt five minutes to explain the deal that night. Edwin cut him off at two minutes.

"I'm in," he told him.

Amelia knew that Edwin had something big to tell her last Christmas, but he'd never gotten the chance.

This is what he wanted to tell her right before the boys went missing.

Edwin bought into the project wholeheartedly, Walt said, but with his unexpected passing, the contract could have been deemed void if not for one key provision. Edwin had listed Amelia Cook as his only employee at the store. Under the terms of the deal, she had the right to assume ownership of the store. This meant assuming its debt as well. Riddell Industries simply cut a check to the bank. Well, several checks. Mr. Z's was now hers.

The store was restocked and ready for business by last February. Business was booming. Mr. Z's franchise stores had already opened in Seattle, Portland and San Francisco. In July the flagship Spokane store closed for one week so Josh and Amelia could spend their first days as husband and wife together somewhere other than Spokane. They took the kids and spent some warm days on the sandy shores of Long Beach, Washington.

Around that same time two men were arrested for seemingly unrelated crimes. A man named Royce Tidau was arrested for killing a security guard in Montana. The chemical stolen during the murder was traced to Spokane and a false natural gas leak. Tidau quickly squealed on a Seattle real estate developer, Lance Massey, whom he claimed was the brains of the operation. Both men were sure to do serious jail time.

* * *

Several of the children from St. Marks arrived at Mr. Z's at exactly 7 p.m., thanks to Pastor Isakson who chaperoned them. The kids were dressed as Mary, Joseph and the wise men. Baby Jesus was there too, being tossed back and forth between Joseph and one of the wise men. Amelia expertly placed the kids in position. They weren't required to move at all, just stay still for two-minute increments so people could take pictures every Saturday morning. It was a fundraiser for the church and advertising for the store.

Amelia walked outside and met Pastor Isakson, Josh, Marcus and Susanna at the curb for the window's first official unveiling. She'd dressed the window to match the manger scene from last year's Christmas play at St. Marks. Yet, she'd taken a few liberties with the painted background scenery to give it that special touch. Just to the right of the manger was Edwin, Mary and the horse Carter. Edwin and Mary were handing out gifts. Mary's gifts came with small gold tags.

First one snowflake, then two, then a thousand more floated down onto the sidewalk before them as they admired the window scene and the kids struggling to stay still in their costumes. It was the first snowfall of the year. Susanna ran around in circles trying to catch them on her tongue. Josh held her and Marcus tight to his side. It was perfect.

Mary and Edwin would be proud of this window display, Amelia was sure of it.

From The Author

There is no way an independent author like me could publish a book without the help of many, many people. This is very true for Don't Wait For Me. First, I must thank my wife, Katie Kolbet, who patiently waited for me to write the book. I'd ask her cryptic questions while never revealing the full scope of the story until she got a chance to read the entire thing. I'm certain that was annoying, but she didn't show it.

A huge thank you goes to my friends Jessie Wuerst and Brandi Smith who served as beta readers. Their edits and comments improved the story in ways I couldn't have imagined. There's an art to providing constructive criticism. They get it.

Karen Caton served as my copy editor and saved me from more mistakes than I care to count. It's great to have such a tremendous resource in the family. I really appreciate her time and work. Of course, any mistakes in the book are mine alone.

Don't Wait For Me was originally intended to be just a short story. But while writing it, I was inspired by my characters—namely Edwin—to tell a more complete story in a novel-length format. It's amazing how they just take over.

You'll notice in the book that the characters often mention fathers. Nearly every character has something to say about his or her own father. This was intentional, but not for any personal reason. My father passed away when I was in elementary school. My mom, Barbara Kolbet Snyder raised my sister, Kim Gortsema, and me alone and we turned out great, just like most of the characters in the novel. But those relationships in the book impact how the characters see things. You'll also notice very strong mothers in the story—that was intentional too.

The name Edwin was in reference to my grandfather, Edward Kolbet. He was a WWII prisoner of war in Germany. He also passed away when I was young. My little troublemaker, Marcus, was named in honor of my uncle Marc Flemming, who provided me encouragement when I published my first novel, Off The Grid, in 2011. Edwin's unnamed uncle, who used to take him to the hockey games in an orange Volkswagen, was a reference to my uncle Larry Malicki, who passed away while I was writing this story. That Volkswagen and trips to the hockey games were pulled from real life.

My villain Royce Tidau has twin nephews, just as I do—Parker and Ryan. My other nasty character eats dinner at Snyder's Steakhouse, a reference to my mom's husband Dave Snyder. A few of the other references to fathers, I'll leave you to discover on your own.

One of the other main characters of the book—Josh—wasn't even supposed to have a speaking role. But he wiggled his way into the finale of the story and I'm glad he did. I named him after my friend Josh DiLuciano who never failed to ask me about my "next book" when he saw me at work. The peer pressure got to me, I guess.

Special thanks to Tim Mair, who helped me troubleshoot my natural gas evacuation scene. I gave him the scenario I was looking at and without a beat, he had ideas and twists I could apply to the scene. You might recognize his description as the unnamed natural gas manager who talks to Edwin on the street.

I'd also like to thank Lisa Lee who helped me understand a few things about horses—and horse terminology that I desperately needed. I've been on a horse, but I can't say I know much about how they work.

I decided to set the story in Spokane because I love Spokane. I'm the typical local who was born, raised and still lives in Spokane. I changed a few locations and names to fit my storyline, but I bet you can recognize several of the places noted in the story. If you're curious, Mr. Z's is not a real place. The corner of Howard Street and Riverside Avenue is actually a surface parking lot. It's the perfect spot for a toy store if you're in the market to build one.

As for Bonners Ferry, I have to apologize to its residents. Nearly every location—including Rocktop Lake—was made up. It's a fine town though, just watch out for those frozen lakes.

To conclude, I'd like to make one request of you the reader—please review this book online. As an independent author, we rely on word of mouth to publicize our work. There is no better validation for an author's work than a third-party review. Please review it on Amazon, Barnes and Noble, CreateSpace, Goodreads, Smashwords, iBooks or wherever you purchased it. It really does matter and I would truly appreciate it.

Thank you for reading this book. I certainly enjoyed writing it and I hope you enjoyed reading it.

-Dan

About The Author

Dan Kolbet lives in Spokane, Washington with his wife and two daughters. He is a former newspaper editor and reporter. Kolbet currently works as a corporate spokesperson for West Coast energy company.

Kolbet's literary works include the corporate espionage thriller, Off The Grid (2011), and Don't Wait For Me (Nov. 2012), a wonderful, but tragic tale of love, loss and new beginnings. Kolbet prides himself on writing stories that invite a reader in and hold their attention. If you enjoy wasted prose and needless opining, look elsewhere.

You can find Kolbet's personal blog at www.dankolbet.com or like his author page on Facebook www.facebook.com/DanKolbetBooks. Follow Kolbet on Twitter: @dankolbet

Made in the USA
Lexington, KY
20 July 2014